You Are the Führer's Unrequited Love

JEAN-NOËL ORENGO

You Are the Führer's Unrequited Love

Translated from French by David Watson

PENGUIN BOOKS

PENGUIN INTERNATIONAL WRITERS

UK | USA | Canada | Ireland | Australia
India | New Zealand | South Africa

Penguin International Writers is part of the Penguin Random House group of companies whose addresses can be found at global.penguinrandomhouse.com.

Penguin Random House UK
One Embassy Gardens, 8 Viaduct Gardens, London SW11 7BW

penguin.co.uk

First published in French as *Vous êtes l'amour malheureux du Führer*, 2024
Published in Great Britain by Penguin International Writers 2026

Copyright © Éditions Grasset & Fasquelle, 2024
English language translation © David Watson, 2026
003

No part of this book may be used or reproduced in any manner for the purpose of training artificial intelligence technologies or systems. In accordance with Article 4(3) of the DSM Directive 2019/790, Penguin Random House expressly reserves this work from the text and data mining exception.

The moral rights of the author and translator have been asserted

Set in 11.25/14pt Dante MT Std
Typeset by Six Red Marbles UK, Thetford, Norfolk
Printed and bound in Great Britain by Clays Ltd, Elcograf S.p.A.

The authorized representative in the EEA is Penguin Random House Ireland, Morrison Chambers, 32 Nassau Street, Dublin D02 YH68

A CIP catalogue record for this book is available from the British Library

ISBN: 978–0–241–74569–4

Penguin Random House is committed to a sustainable future for our business, our readers and our planet. This book is made from Forest Stewardship Council® certified paper.

Love at First Sight

(1930–1933)

I

Munich, July 1933

The first time that the architect saw the Führer, he was sitting at a table, absorbed in cleaning a pistol. Adolf Hitler – the Führer, the guide – arranged the dismantled parts of the gun and told Albert Speer – the architect, the artist – to place his drawings on the table. They were plans for the second rally of the National Socialist Party since coming to power, due to be held the following year. It would involve a lot of staging, with a rostrum, lighting, tiered stands. For the architect, this was his first major commission. Previously he had redesigned a number of party buildings and decorated the apartment of the minister of education and propaganda, Joseph Goebbels. That early success had led to him heading up this very important project. But no one dared give him the go-ahead. After a while he was sent to Munich, where the guide was in summer residence. Only he could decide whether his work should proceed or not.

At no point did the guide look at him. But he scrutinized his plans very closely. Then, without raising his eyes, in a flat, neutral tone, he said: 'Agreed.'

The meeting was at an end. The architect was dismissed without another word. Then the guide was able to return to flossing, greasing and cleaning the parts of his pistol, the exact make of which is unknown.

2

This opening scene is borrowed from biographers of Albert Speer, who themselves borrowed it from the man himself.

Some novels play around with chronology, using flashback and anticipation as part of their technical arsenal, and we must now commit a similar offence and disrupt the comfortable linear flow of the narrative.

Albert Speer survived the war, and in a manner of speaking he also survived his own personal history, which brought him close to death on more than one occasion. He writes about all this in *Inside the Third Reich*, his bestselling memoirs, published in 1969. The book brought him a form of respectability, relative financial security and an unsettling public image, which made him unique among former leading Nazis who openly displayed their past. Since its publication, his book has exceeded its genre and become something else entirely. Some junior SS officers and military and political chiefs from the regime have also brought out their own memoirs, but in comparison they enjoyed only minor success, and historians have had little difficulty in separating the image they projected of themselves from the reality.

With Albert Speer, it was different. He managed to impose his own self-image despite the counter-versions produced by historians and researchers, with the result that, paradoxically, biographies of him often read like rewrites of his own memoirs.

This is not plagiarism. The historians were in the front line of the battle against the source text; they were armed with documents that revealed the lies and omissions, but in the end the truth failed to win the day and Speer came out on top.

He seems to have waged an unprecedented war over his narrative, a war which only he was able to fight, because of his relationship with Hitler and his expertise in art and military production, two disciplines in which it is rare for a single individual to excel. A master of design and of armaments, he has put himself forward as a key witness, simultaneously spectator and actor, with Adolf Hitler and his court in the foreground. In the background – and it is a background of horror – he claimed that the extermination of the Jews of Europe, as we now know it, was something he was unaware of during its unfolding, only discovering it from 1945 onwards, which sets up an undeniable and unwholesome dramatic tension.

Written in the late 1960s, and dealing with an event that occurred in 1933, the scene of their meeting is told in simple, basic terms, with few details. Yet these details are striking and incisive, like a chess move.

Two men, alone in a room; a pistol; a drawing.

Power on one side, art on the other.

On the one side, the man of power – his weapon lying in front of him – on the other, the man of art – his drawings under his arm. A typical pairing of European culture. They could be Julius II and Michelangelo. They are Adolf Hitler and Albert Speer.

And it was in this counterbalance of forces that their relationship was born.

3

There is something highly improbable about this first professional meeting, the purpose of which is no less than the major political rally of the new regime. Almost a postwar caricature in that it brilliantly shows a Führer *rearming* himself.

Adolf Hitler attached the utmost importance to visual and aural manifestations of National Socialist ideology. It was he who chose the swastika as the emblem of his movement, a criminal embezzlement that continues to this day, the perversion of a universal and benevolent symbol in many cultures, principally in India and Southeast Asia, that has become synonymous with massacre and racial hatred.

In 1933, the guide had yet to settle on satisfactory ways to symbolize and represent the new regime. He was looking for someone. And he was not just a head of state.

It is impossible today to understand the attraction Adolf Hitler was able to exert on German and even foreign crowds during the 1920s and 1930s. All his biographers come face to face with this impossibility. Given the scale of the crimes committed, it is not adequate to attribute this attraction to societal alibis such as the economic crisis or the pervasive antisemitism of the time. And the person himself seems inexplicable from an existential point of view. Neither an abusive father, nor a frustrating youth, let alone so-called revelations about his sexuality or anatomy, serve to explain the gas chambers. The extermination of

Europe's Jews split history in two. Albert Speer seems to have known this sooner than the others, or at least he knew better how to rationalize this separation and use it.

When his daughter wrote to him one day to ask him to give an account of himself, in the same way that millions of German children questioned why their parents had hailed Hitler as their Führer, he replied that 'the enormity of the crime makes any attempt to justify it null and void'.

Neither Speer's personal ambition, nor a lack of paternal recognition, nor indeed anything else can completely explain the relationship between him and his guide.

What is certain is that he had just met the most photographed man in Germany, and one of the most photographed in the world. Fame had become a major currency of post-1918 societies. By 1933, the guide was – along with Gandhi – the most mediated political animal on the planet. Apart from a few writers and filmmakers in exile, who were barely taken seriously, perhaps only Winston Churchill, in a 1934 article, could foresee the consequences of his racial obsessions for the law and politics of an advanced country like Germany. For many, his antisemitism was not much different from their own, or could at least be dismissed as a necessary side-effect of his attempts to reconstruct his country. The communists underestimated him and mocked him; Gertude Stein, the Jewish American lesbian novelist, lobbied for him to be given the Nobel Peace Prize, and Charlie Chaplin spotted the undeniable genius in his dramatic speeches. A star.

By way of a welcome, the guide left the young architect wrestling with a series of contradictory emotions.

He left the guide's office happy but taken aback, frustrated by his indifference, perplexed, proud at having his drawings endorsed, disappointed not to have made any personal contact. He found it impossible to set his emotions in any order, something he had never experienced before. Whether pleasant or unpleasant, the feelings were strong and unfamiliar. At that time, music was exploring *atonality*, the absence of tonality, of hierarchy of scale, which for listeners educated on centuries of harmony generated a feeling of uneasiness, aural destabilization, disharmony, as well as of fascination and sonic intoxication. Face to face with the guide, something identical occurred. An amoral and unsentimental experience, where one could no longer order one's feelings. Anger, fear, love of one's own, hatred of others, all merged in a set of quite primitive emotions, archetypes found in every society that feels under threat.

The Führer was an atonal creature, just as he was an expressionist creature, a character drawn from the paintings and musical scores of his time, he who hated expressionism and atonality and persecuted the painters, musicians and poets belonging to these movements. He was an entirely unique figure, who had developed an irresistible physical style where the violence of his words, his duplicity, his eloquence and his deportment made him judge everything all at once as ridiculous, intelligent, vulgar, modern, visionary, mediumistic, pacifist, reassuring, disturbing . . . a whole gamut of extreme, conflicting emotions and judgements, in a heady, repetitive atmosphere, speech after speech recycling his restricted range of themes indefinitely.

This guide had just extended to the architect the hand most desired by an artist, that of the sponsor, of the patron of the arts. And yet he remained coldly focused on the dismantled parts of a pistol.

4

Doubtless a Walther PP. Or perhaps its more compact version, a Walther PPK. A German bestseller. The guide owned a number of these. On 30 April 1945, he probably used one to put a bullet in his own head; it has now disappeared, perhaps the keepsake of some family in the former Soviet Union. It was they, the Soviets, the soldiers of the glorious Red Army, who would be the first to enter Berlin and the famous Führer bunker, which has been recreated meticulously by generations of filmmakers obsessed with the last days of the guide and his court. One of the Red soldiers must have helped himself to this gun, already a relic, already tarnished with an unhealthy and legendary patina for this very reason. There are many articles about this on the internet. Along with pornography, Nazism generates a huge number of online searches. And in this morass of articles of varying academic quality, there is much discussion of the Walther PPK hypothesis among internet enthusiasts of the Second World War and the Third Reich. But it's still guesswork. The details are missing.

Details are of course important. Think of the opening words of Marx's *Capital*: 'The wealth of societies under the capitalist mode of production takes the form of an enormous accumulation of commodities.' The historian, the novelist and the poet function in the same way.

That is, the wealth of a text under the historical, poetic or novelistic mode of writing takes the form of an enormous accumulation of details.

The architect didn't really add much detail or decoration when he made his drawings for the 1933 rally. Some very tall and very long swastika banners spaced along the back of a long platform. A giant eagle posed in the centre, wings outstretched. Wood and fabric, basically quite fragile materials not designed to last for centuries. For the guide, it seems that this was enough and he did not need any further information or to engage in conversation with its creator. In fact it seems that, contrary to appearances, the guide knew the architect already and hadn't forgotten him.

5

Germany, October 1932

The first time the guide encountered the architect was through his work, which he admired. Modest, but highly promising. He visited the new Party headquarters in Berlin in the autumn of 1932. It was a late nineteenth-century building, typical of the period, somewhat pompous in style. Façades overloaded with cornices, cherubs, friezes and caryatids. Hitler considered the second half of the nineteenth century as a golden era of art – and for him art meant architecture, music, painting and sculpture above all – literature passed him by entirely. Wasn't Richard Wagner the greatest German composer? Wasn't he a typical man of the nineteenth century? He was keen on Wagner's pet notion of total art. There was also the cinema, which was his night-time passion: he would organize long, exhausting screenings for his court. He was a night owl, rarely turning in before four or five in the morning and often not until dawn.

Looking at the architect's renovation work, which decluttered the things that needed to go – dusty drapes and disgusting carpets – in order to bring out the height of the walls, and to highlight some of the decorative elements that had been preserved, such as stucco and woodwork, he perceived an aptitude for the monumental that immediately beguiled him. He shared his enthusiasm with his entourage. It is possible that he probed more closely into the architect's personal history without his knowledge.

According to Speer's memoirs, the guide was unaware of certain facts of the young man's life; as the latter revealed them to him when their relationship developed, he met with astonishment, confusion and even a certain enchantment in his master. And he is doubtless sincere in his recollections.

However, this version of events barely stands up. At the time of their first meeting, Reichsführer-SS Heinrich Himmler had already built an excellent internal intelligence service. It kept precise records on anyone who held or aspired to hold office in the Party, the state, the media, industry, banking, science, the arts. It was a huge bureaucratic machine, producing spectacular amounts of paperwork. Of course, Hitler was no bureaucrat. He very rarely read files, of any sort. But he received oral reports. It is not impossible that he spoke to the SS about this tall, thin, young architect.

This would better explain his attitude in those first few months. It was as if he always had a head start in their relationship, a mixture of hot and cold, above all a flattering astonishment at what this other man was revealing to him about his life.

Given their factual nature, reports can sometimes read like a dictionary or Wikipedia entry, but in a novel you can distort facts by suggesting parallels that would be considered unscientific in other contexts.

6

The guide was listening to an SS officer in his office, around 1932.

Albert Speer was a German citizen of Aryan stock. To date, no Jewish blood had been detected in his family tree. He was born on 19 March 1905 in Mannheim, in the west of the country. His family were not rich or influential, but he wasn't no one either, like the Führer – *the SS man did not say this out loud, but perhaps did so inwardly, a sort of inner monologue or stream of consciousness that some avant-garde novels of the time were experimenting with, he was no doubt himself a graduate, a Doctor of Law or Medicine, many SS men in the service were, they belonged to the well-to-do bourgeoisie who were ruined or impoverished by the 1929 crash, they had the reflexes of their class and a careerist opportunism that would no longer be evident in the younger SS members who had grown up with Nazism – they were total fanatics and totally incapable of any silent irony vis-à-vis their Führer.*

His father was an architect. His grandfather was an architect. He was from the upper middle class. Since 1918 they had resided in Heidelberg, in what used to be their second home. They had servants, they owned cars. Their neighbours had nothing negative to say about them. They owned properties that brought in substantial amounts of rent. Albert Speer didn't have to work. He was like a character in a Thomas Mann novel – *the SS man didn't make this remark either, Thomas Mann was not a Nazi sympathizer, and yet this young Albert Speer was a typical Buddenbrook character, with one notable difference: he was not a decadent like the ultimate scion of Mann's novel. He was perfectly healthy, tall, slim, cold and aloof, though friendly, according to his friends, a description exactly matching the one the guide had given recently in a speech about the German of the future, who, in his eyes,* 'must be lithe, slender, quick as a greyhound, solid as leather and hard as Krupp steel'. He was, or had been, a rower, rugby player, skier, mountaineer and hiker – he knew the *Wanderweg*, the walking trail, well, that very German topological and linguistic trope. The great romantic Germany of the forests and the peaks, he knew it by heart, in his heart and in his legs. He was tall. He was thin. He dressed well. He wore a double-breasted suit well. He had the hands of an artist. He had a strong aptitude for mathematics. He had wanted to be a mathematician. He became an architect in deference to his father. It had done him no harm to obey his father. He had been brought up to show obedience to teachers and father figures. He was not a man who was a danger to women, because they weren't especially important in his life. He had met a girl, Margarete – Margret for short – when he was seventeen, a German girl of Aryan stock the same age as him. They had married on 28 August 1928. He was not known to have had any affairs. He was no skirt-chaser – *just like you, my Führer, you are almost abnormally monogamous, given the mass of love letters sent to you by our sisters, our daughters, our mothers and even our girlfriends, to whom you always give the same response: I am married to Germany.* He taught at the technical college in Berlin, where he himself had studied architecture under a certain Heinrich Tessenow. He had become his assistant. He had joined the NSDAP on 1 March 1931, and his membership number was 474 481. More remarkably, his mother was also a member. The guide had always worshipped his own mother.

7

The SS man summarized another file. This one was on the aforementioned Heinrich Tessenow. The guide wanted more information on this architect whom this tall, slim young man worked for. He was a German citizen of Aryan stock. He was old. He was born on 7 April 1878 in Rostock. He was old Germany – and the guide hated old Germany. Tessenow the architect was a modernist. He favoured glass, concrete and the skeletal lines of modernism. The guide hated concrete, glass and the skeletal lines of those buildings that were dead before they had even lived. The young architect was connected to this man, this old German typical of a Germany that the guide would destroy for ever. That was not important. Tessenow was neither a Jew nor a communist. He was no one. True, he had adopted Jewish tastes. True, Nazi students had heckled him because of his somewhat internationalist tendencies, his penchant for concrete and glass. But when he was faced with protests by other students, the Party had sent him a form letter assuring him of the esteem in which he was held.

In the months that followed, the guide kept an eye on the young architect's progress. He himself had an architectural mentor. His name was Paul Troost. He was from Munich – the guide adored Munich. They had met in 1929. He was an old German of Aryan stock born in 1878, very tall, very strong, an old professor who embodied eternal Germany, a neoclassical Germany, a Graeco-Roman Germany, a slightly Latin Germany, not particularly Germanic, not gothic or Wagnerian, but the guide was untroubled by the contradictions, even though he venerated Wagner and had meticulously reproduced several gothic cathedrals in his youthful paintings. There were lots of columns with Troost; no ornamentation, everything was smooth, angular, massive, without domes or friezes or eloquent curves. But he hadn't always been like this. At one point he had even been in bed with modernism. He had flirted with certain members of the Bauhaus – the guide hated Bauhaus. In particular, he had fitted out some cruise liners in Streamline Moderne style: simple, functional, comfortable furniture, with sober curves, rounded corners, a sub-type of Art Nouveau in the tree of decorative styles. The guide consistently addressed Paul Troost as *Herr Professor*.

The young architect's rise went hand in hand with that of the Party.

In January 1933, the Nazis were invited to form a government. He was happy.

In March, he refurbished the building of the newly created Ministry of Education and Propaganda led by Joseph Goebbels, one of the Führer's inner circle. Still in March, he rubbished plans for a rally with a speech by the guide on the esplanade of Tempelhof airport in Berlin and was challenged to come up with something better. The next day, he suggested a long rostrum surmounted with gigantic swastika flags illuminated by massive searchlights. The rally took place on 1 May and was a huge success; the guide was enthused by the staging.

In June, he refurbished Goebbels' apartment at lightning speed. The guide had been sceptical, he had a playful bet with his minister. He and his close friends liked betting at the expense of one or other of their subordinates; it was a parlour game for them, and they often made cruel jokes to put them down. The young architect brought it off on time, and the guide was curious to see the result. He thought he had done an excellent job, apart from the paintings on the walls, the work of a certain Emil Nolde. He was a German citizen of Aryan stock, an ardent admirer of Nazism and the guide, and a pure antisemite who launched diatribes against the Jews worthy of the crudest jibes of the SA. He belonged to the so-called 'expressionist' movement, which portrayed distorted, disgusting caricatural figures in place of the beautiful neoclassical ephebes and caryatids favoured by the guide. The guide hated expressionism and was scandalized to see it in the home of his minister, who was proud of his avant-garde tastes. This Nolde painted like a Jew, so he was a German of Jewified stock. A Jew disguised as a German of Aryan stock. A Jewish Nazi! 'We decide who is Jewish,' Goebbels reportedly told the filmmaker Fritz Lang, Ashkenazi on his mother's side, whom he was trying to convince to stay in the new Germany. They also decided who had the right to be a Nazi. Nolde was an expressionist, so he was not a good Nazi. A lack of taste and a crime against art that Goebbels picked up on immediately, incriminating Speer as he did so. The guide shrugged his shoulders. It wasn't important.

Goebbels treated the young architect with relative indifference. He paid him no more attention than any other; their relationship was one of boss and subordinate. He was an architect but not the only one, there were more and more of these in the Party, just as there were more and more lawyers and doctors joining, three professions massively seduced by the Nazi programmes on race, law and construction. Goebbels indiscreetly repeated to his entourage, who repeated it to Speer, the guide's enthusiasm for his various achievements over the past year at Tempelhof and the Ministry of Propaganda, and his explosive hatred of Nolde's paintings.

The architect took all this in, learned from it and adapted immediately. No one had praised him like this, certainly not Tessenow, and the fact that it was the most powerful man in Germany filled him with joy.

They agreed more than they disagreed. Deep down, he wasn't sure whether he liked expressionism or not. It was all the same to him. For example, he saw himself as a music lover, he liked to attend concerts, he knew conductors and prestigious musicians, whom he evokes briefly but admiringly in his memoirs. But he never mentioned Anton Webern, Igor Stravinsky, Alban Berg or Arnold Schoenberg, names it would be absurd to omit if you had a genuine interest in music. To all appearances, he was like those bourgeois young men brought up in the 1920s who were obsessed with not missing the latest big thing and who wanted to distinguish themselves from their parents and grandparents, who had looked down on impressionism, fauvism, Gauguin, Van Gogh and all the geniuses of the last quarter of the nineteenth century and the first part of the twentieth century. But in fact, in this social milieu, love of the arts was more a matter of convention than conviction. Painting and music were more to do with entertainment than anything else, which meant that there were none of those polemical and passionate discussions that the real music lovers and art lovers indulged in. They were at best a form of decorum.

He was a master of the art of decorum, on whatever scale, whether an apartment or a rally, just as the guide was a master of manipulating an audience through his voice, whatever the scale, collective or individual.

The young architect could vouch for that, and he would do so for the rest of his life, even when he condescendingly disowned the guide. He had become a Nazi in a single evening, because of that voice and the visions it evoked.

8

Germany, December 1930

The first time that the architect saw the Führer was at a rally in a hall in a public park. More importantly, it was the first time he heard him. This was in Berlin in December 1930, during the Weimar Republic, in the era of the noxious 'System'.

Both communists and Nazis called the Weimar Republic the 'System' and they would always refer to it this way: the 'System', with its rotten machinery, its mixture of softness towards criminals and authoritarianism when it came to honest workers, concealing the worst form of dictatorship, the dictatorship of democrats who had sold out to *them*, the Americans, the Jews, the bosses, the global oligarchy of banks and trusts. The Nazis would never forget this in the corridors of their new power, even when they themselves became immensely rich. They would constantly remind everyone that Germans of Aryan stock suffered under the 'System' more than Germans of foreign or Jewish stock. You only had to go to the cabarets and nightclubs of Berlin, Hanover or Düsseldorf, that racy nocturnal world of Weimar Germany, to see beautiful but impoverished Aryan women flashing their bare breasts and long legs to a mishmash of pseudo-German wops, all pot-bellied, bloated, ruddy-cheeked, mouths stinking of cigars, ogling through their monocles.

The architect was quietly vegetating in his vaguely professorial life, more precisely his role as Professor Tessenow's assistant at the technical college in Berlin, unaware of what his future might hold. He didn't frequent cabarets or nightclubs, he was already a respectable married man; he shared with his wife a taste for the *Wanderweg*, donning backpacks to take long walks in the forests and mountains of Germany. But he was waiting for something. He just didn't know what.

Once again, it is he who tells us all this, long after the event, in the form of a confession that is difficult to verify. No matter, the picture he draws is one that corresponds to the zeitgeist that historians and novelists attribute to the 1930s, a mixture of extreme social crises and political messianism.

One evening, his students twisted his arm to come and listen to an extraordinary man. Many had signed up to the guide's party; young people idolized him. The architect was familiar with this Hitler and his free-flowing speeches; they hadn't grabbed his attention all that much. He found the unfiltered hate speech distasteful, and this put him off listening further. This sort of thing didn't appeal to people like him, especially the pseudo-military uniform, which had nothing of the dignity of the real thing. The architect was antisemitic, of course, in a way that was very common throughout Europe and the United States. For him it was convention rather than genuine conviction, and he would later write in a letter that he had nothing against the Jews apart from a level of discomfort in their presence. He spoke to them in a courteous and respectful manner as he would to anyone. Deep down, he was indifferent to the Jews; he felt neither positive nor negative towards them.

He attended the meeting out of curiosity, so as not to miss out on the latest thing. The hall was packed when he arrived.

You Are the Führer's Unrequited Love

Several thousand young people with their somewhat older teachers. Aside from the mass rallies, the guide often addressed more specialized audiences like this. On this winter evening, it was almost like an event with the author of a bestseller. Which is what he became. Published in 1925, *Mein Kampf* was beginning to sell in large numbers.

He appeared on the podium dressed in an elegant double-breasted suit offsetting that much-photographed moustache and hairline, which appealed to his admirers as much as his detractors. He looked emotionally charged, focused. The architect had not really followed his speeches broadcast on the radio; he had often come in halfway through one of his characteristic and embarrassing tirades, a stentorian, serious-sounding monologue full of threats and antisemitic hatred. At first he was stupefied by the tone of that voice, a sort of hesitation and humility before the magnitude of the subjects covered – art, the incomparable importance of the arts to civilization. He seemed to place politics at the service of the arts rather than vice versa. He said that a state, a country exists only through the traces left by its monuments, its sculptures, its paintings, its music. He raised his voice when he talked about present-day decadence, the financial and spiritual impoverishment of all these frustrated unemployed young artists deprived of greatness in a regime with purely prosaic and mercantile ambitions. He attacked the Jews, but only in passing, and it was the riff about his love of art that stuck in the architect's head. It was full of platitudes, but convoluted subtleties had led to nothing in the Germany of 1930. It was full of truisms, but every spectacle starts with a truism. For example, a dome, with its arches, its coffers, its curves, its acoustics, has been an architectural truism for millennia, but once it is built, it is an object of rapture for the public. It is irresistible, it works for ever. Delicate types may well shrug their shoulders, the dome will crush delicacy with its effects every time.

At the end of the meeting, there was a torrent of applause, outpourings of enthusiasm, a crush to get an autograph and exchange a few words with the guide.

The architect was stunned. He didn't rejoin his students, he left the hall immediately, got in his car and spent the night meditating profoundly on the moonlit sky next to the Havel, a river that passed through west Berlin in the district of Spandau. It could have been a scene from a Goethe play – '*I come beneath your shades, swaying treetops of the ancient, sacred wood, thick with leaves*' – or a painting by Caspar David Friedrich; it was a 1930 landscape but it illustrated the eternal romanticism of Germany. Romanticism was what made Germany universal, especially for young people, of whatever era or nationality. The architect's life was lived under the sign of German romanticism. That was his best defence, and he never wavered from it.

For nearly three years, they met on numerous occasions without ever speaking, unconsciously observing and admiring each other. The guide no doubt knew more about the architect than he would let on later, but he didn't realize to what extent he had signed up to his monumental visions. And the architect didn't know whether the positive things the guide said about him were sincere or simply throwaway remarks.

Autumn 1933. The guide was now the undisputed master of Germany. The architect was commissioned to refurbish the residence of the Reich chancellor, which stank of a certain type of mould, the mould of the old Germany. It was in fact Troost who drew up the plans, but he was in Munich; Speer was familiar with Berlin and its building firms, so he oversaw the works.

The guide came almost every day to visit the building site. While work was underway, he was living in a tiny apartment upstairs. He was very pleasant with the workers, chatting with them, but never with the architect. He ignored him. The architect accepted this and concentrated his energies on carrying out his mission.

Then one day, out of the blue, the guide invited him to lunch.

Honeymoon

(1933–1934)

9

The young architect was surprised, discombobulated. He had just splashed plaster on his jacket, he wasn't presentable. He was taken aback, stunned, happy, tense, worried about this sudden invitation.

The guide reassured him, looked him up and down, sized him up. True, the architect was taller than him, but the difference was negligible – the guide was not short despite what his opponents said about him. One metre seventy-five is a decent height; often in parades only his SS guards were taller than him. The guide immediately sent for one of his own jackets, held it against him. It suited him well. The jacket sported a gold pin with an eagle holding a swastika in its claws. It was the Führer's insignia, and no one else was allowed to wear it. The guide asked the young architect to follow him into the dining room.

A double surprise for the guests. Most of them didn't know this young man walking in behind their Führer. He was slim and tall – one metre eighty-two – and they were all shorter and older. It was the first time he had been in this company, and he was wearing the Führer's insignia. Goebbels was especially surprised, not to say furious. He couldn't rein in his indignation and incomprehension and pointed out to Speer that he was wearing the Führer's insignia. The guide responded curtly that he had given him the jacket himself. And he sat the architect next to him.

Still, the difference in height was not inconsiderable. One metre eighty-two and one metre seventy-five are not the same thing. So it is odd that Hitler's jacket fitted Speer so well. In his memoirs, the jacket fitted him like a glove and, symbolically, anointed him as the Führer's successor. By 1969, all the other witnesses of this lunch were dead. Speer was alone with his memories.

During the meal, they formed a little clique apart from the rest of the guests. The guide plied him with questions about his family, his father and grandfather, both architects, and their projects. He listened. He was surprised. He discovered that it was he, this young architect, who was behind the astonishing design of the rally at Tempelhof on 1 May 1933. It was as if he were finding this out for the first time. So that was you! It was a real piece of political theatre. Unmatched to this day. Maybe earlier, in Rome. Yes, definitely, the triumphs after a victory over the barbarians. Hollywood portrayed them quite well, he had to admit. Did the architect – the artist – like cinema? Did he like westerns? Did he like epics? Did he like comedies with pretty actresses? The guide adored cinema. Would the architect like to come and see a film one evening, when the residence was finished? In any case, it had been a whole new level of scenography, the 1 May rally at Tempelhof. Even the Bolsheviks, with their parades in Moscow, couldn't match it. They couldn't create such effects. The communists had no artistic sensibility. The communists had no grasp of the relationship of politics and the fine arts. The guide could show him his own drawings, his own architectural plans. They could get together again in a more serious setting and exchange ideas about all this.

10

Later, just before the war, probably at Obersalzberg, on one of those walks when they were photographed together, the guide confided in the young architect. Obersalzberg, the Berghof, the guide's residence in the Bavarian Alps. It might equally have been in the living room, with its large bay window overlooking the mountains, a décor more than a landscape, framed as if on a cinema screen. But they were rarely alone together in this cosy space, always surrounded by courtesans. So it was more likely out on a forest *Wanderweg*, high in the mountains, breath steaming as they talked. The guide had a leash in his hand, leather gloves and boots, he was walking Blonda, one of his beloved dogs. Behind them, some distance back, were other members of his circle and friends. The guide was silent. The architect was silent. They had their eyes fixed on the path in front of them. They wore military caps which further obscured their expressions. They had been ruminating over their sketches for a gigantic dome and a gigantic triumphal arch. And now they walked in silence, contemplating their dreams of stone.

Suddenly, the guide broke the silence and in a low, serious voice said: 'I noticed you during my inspection visits. I was looking for an architect that I could entrust with my projects. He must be young, because, as you know, these are very long-term projects. I need someone who will be able to continue my work after my death with the authority I will bestow on him. That man is you.'

II

With this lunch, the architect entered the Führer's inner circle. Magic words for its members. To be chosen to be by his side. It is a phenomenon common to all powerful figures. The architect knew this, he wasn't naive. Even in his own milieu, at the technical college of Berlin with Tessenow, he had experience of all the manoeuvring required to obtain a post and elbow out the other candidates. Joining the inner circle of a president, a captain of industry, a Führer, involved the same ambitions and the same intrigues. Deference, obsequiousness, sycophancy, submission, fear, the tension of seduction, always seduction – this was the emotional repertoire of the courtier. Behind the scenes of a board of directors at a large company or a prestigious university, you grovelled before the masters, your star rose or fell in the same way as in the antechambers of a dictatorship. In the case of the guide, this banal truism of power was massively amplified. It was on a different scale, and the moral consequences were different too. The guide spoke, and his close circle vied with each other to interpret his mostly verbal pronouncements, each in their own way, in the form of written orders.

But also, indisputably, there is such a thing as love at first sight. There are cases, especially in politics and art, where two individuals see something in each other beyond prosaic ambitions or the competition for financial or personal gain. Fine art and politics reflect and attract one another, and from the Pyramids to the palaces of popes and kings, architecture has always been the main locus of their encounter. But here too, in the case of Speer and Hitler, the scale and the moral consequences were of a different order.

The guide practised a sort of art of contrast. For the architect, there was a huge difference between the private and the public man. He seemed as amicable on the inside as he came across as authoritarian and implacable on the outside. It was a theatrical effect, a contrast that was stark but irresistible to the architect. An aesthetic experience at the very heart of power similar to what in music is known as chromatism and in painting as chiaroscuro, but without any nuance. The guide's intimacy acted as a counterpoint to his authority. You felt that you had been selected by the chosen one, chosen by him, the man of power, you sat at his table, received his confidences, you were alone with him, you were different because of him. It was an emotional divide; when you shared one of his meals, you counterbalanced this with the thought of all those from the inner circle who were not sharing it.

It was a circle, like an engagement ring was a circle. Entering it was like feeling a ring on your finger.

From now on, the architect was breathing the air of another planet.

He rented an artist's studio a few hundred metres from the Chancellery. He wanted to be available at a moment's notice if summoned by the man he called 'my sponsor'. He had made an important discovery about himself. He was more madly in love with work than with any person. Married life didn't offer him the same feelings. Other people in different professions sometimes make a similar discovery. When he was in his studio, he wasn't working, he was living. Physically, the work engaged him more than when he made love with his wife. After he met the guide, he was away from home more and more.

This work was not abstract. It was embodied in the guide. When the architect was in his studio designing and above all organizing various renovations of old buildings for the Party's use, the work was Hitler – the guide, the Führer.

And the commissions built up. To fulfil them he put together a team of men, exclusively men, all of them young. That was a criterion of selection. They were young, and the architect praised and appreciated their devotion to work at the expense of their private lives. From morning until evening, day after day, they worked feverishly, and the guide would visit frequently. Their youth was devoted to the architect, and he was devoted to the guide.

12

'Gloomy!' That was the guide's comment on the newly renovated home of his minister-president of Prussia, Reichstag president, minister of aviation and old fellow traveller Hermann Göring. He perused the house coldly. How could you live in such a place, all these shabby little rooms, like some tiny flat or a dolls' house, these windows with their heavy curtains, the floor space crammed with even heavier furniture? And all these grotesque nooks and crannies, these alcoves, and this overabundance of couches, as if in readiness for some impromptu declaration, and consummation, of passionate love to one of those ambiguous creatures the minister-president of Prussia, president of the Reichstag, minister of aviation and old fellow traveller Hermann Göring was particularly and disastrously fond of? And then all those swastikas. They were maybe the worst. They were everywhere: on the walls, the floor, the cushions. It was like a child drawing hearts to win the love of its parents. It was unworthy of a man of his status. So yes, it was very 'gloomy'.

At one of those lunches of the inner circle, Göring asked his Führer – like everyone he called him 'my Führer', except that with his voice, his uniforms, his excessive obsequiousness this already pompous martial epithet sounded even more infantile and caricatural – whether it was Speer who had designed his splendid personal apartment. The guide replied in the affirmative. He was lying, it wasn't him. Speer was just Troost's project manager, but he said yes. Göring asked permission to employ Speer to redesign his own home. The guide said yes, without seeking the young man's agreement, but he was delighted. Speer belonged to him and he showed that to everyone by offering him to Göring without asking him first, and for the architect it was a privilege and a pleasure to belong to him.

After the meal, Göring drove him in his beautiful flashy convertible to his 'gloomy' apartment – the architect was in complete agreement with the guide. He said that he couldn't stand it any more, and there was now only one condition: that it should be 'like the Führer's place'.

Interior decorator, that's what I am right now, thought the architect. He flitted between the palaces of the potentates of the new regime, like this Göring. He knocked down partition walls, made large ceremonial spaces, accentuated the heights and perspectives common to these buildings, allowing the light in, playing with shadows. His scenic approach, his skill in creating an opera-like ambience, was very popular.

But ultimately he was a domestic set designer for the elite. Was that so bad? He had become part of the inner circle of the leader of Germany, something unimaginable just a few months earlier. The problem was, it wasn't enough for him any more. The problem was that frequenting the guide fired his euphoria about architecture. Architecture was the power of space. All architects are authoritarian and perfectly aware that they dictate our living spaces with their constructions. More than painters, musicians or sculptors, and beyond compare with writers or dancers, modern architects played the role of 'artists' for politicians. But with the guide this cliché was raised to another level. He saw himself as an artist-chancellor, the state's architect-in-chief. In architecture, he valued wild ambition, as seen in his sketches for triumphal arches or domes that must always – a cast-iron rule – be larger than anything that went before. It was as if he were fighting a war against the architecture of other nations and those of the past, even the past of Germany. A war of monuments and a war of signs, the swastika fighting on the terrain of the Christian crucifix, not to mention the hammer and sickle, a vulgar, deracinated insignia, according to the guide. With him, the architect thought, stone, signs and their effects contained the promise of unprecedented sensations and dimensions. The promise of power.

13

Since becoming a member of the inner circle, the architect had been taking great delight in the rituals of his new life.

Meals were a big part of it. Being invited was not necessarily connected to your rank in the Party or the government. In fact, it was a circle made up of a number of different circles, but not like ripples in the water; these circles were nowhere near as placid.

For example, there was Heinrich Himmler's circle, though he hardly ever turned up, preferring to spend his time with his mysterious sect, the SS.

There was the circle of Hermann Göring, who came less and less.

'The food there is very poor,' he said one day to Speer, 'and all these old hangers-on around the Führer are just the old Munich petty bourgeoisie!'

There was the Rudolf Hess circle. He was the secretary of the Reich Chancellery and was also the guide's secretary when he wrote his bestseller, *Mein Kampf*. Hess had increasingly become persona non grata. He had some unfortunate tics, such as bringing his own food when visiting the guide – a bizarre vegetarian variant known as the biodynamic diet, which was based on spiritual beliefs involving the presence of nymphs in rivers and springs, and all kinds of elvish spirits and goblins in plants and trees. The architect was there when the guide noticed

Hess's bowls being heated up in the kitchen, which put his nose permanently out of joint.

There was Joseph Goebbels' circle. He frequently attended lunches or dinners despite his busy social life. He was one of the most sharp-tongued of the guests. The guide adored him because he made jokes at other people's expense.

And then there was Martin Bormann, who was a circle unto himself. Officially, he was the secretary of Rudolph Hess, who was himself the Chancellery secretary. But with Hess being more and more absent, he was the one who effectively did the work. He was constantly at the guide's side. He organized his money. He organized his appointments. He organized his travel. He organized Obersalzberg, as members of the circle often wanted to stay there. He organized lunches, and requests from courtiers to be invited. He ran a waiting list, except for Göring, Goebbels, Himmler, Speer and a few others, who had unfettered access, especially Speer, whom the guide could no longer do without.

There were some familiar faces from the early days: Sepp Dietrich, the Führer's head bodyguard, Julius Schreck, his driver. They both had moustaches like the guide's. The architect found that disturbing and weird, though he always had a soft spot for Sepp Dietrich, especially when he became the general of an SS Panzer army and in 1942 married a beautiful and elegant woman who was very café society chic; they were the quintessential Beauty and the Beast. By then, he had shaved off the moustache.

And then there were various nonentities: the head of the Chancellery press office, a doctor and surgeon available 24/7 in case of any medical problem and a few one-off visitors, old Party comrades whom the guide tolerated less and less because they were familiar with him in a way that was no longer fitting to his new duties. Not so much duties as prophetic missions in the fields of armament, foreign policy, domestic policy, racial policy, not to mention the art of the Third Reich. Many of these nonentities were members of the SA, headed by Ernst Röhm, whose vulgar manners increasingly grated on the guide.

The architect noted the internal divisions and jealousies of each of these groups, but he did so without appearing to, his mind apparently elsewhere, entirely filled with art, which the guide valued so much. This lofty, detached attitude suited him well, an attitude typical of an 'artist', a fictional character rather than the real artist who diverted, fascinated and irritated those men of power.

Be that as it may, when the guide had people for lunch, Bormann got everyone to pay for their meal. It would cost 50 or 100 Marks. The Third Reich wasn't the 'System': *we don't fill our bellies at the taxpayers' expense*, it always amused him to say.

14

The guide's days were repetitive. He got up late, went to bed late, the meals went on for ever, the work suffered.

It was a serial sort of existence, where the same topics of discussion were rehashed in various thematic combinations rarely troubled by current events – the Night of the Long Knives, the Anschluss, matters which were now merely a dim and distant backdrop of their circle, especially for the architect.

1933, 1938, 1936: the dates tended to merge into each other in this repetitive existence where time was suspended. They had lunch at two in the afternoon, went their separate ways around four or five, met up again at eight, waited for the guide to turn up, he came, they had dinner, they chatted, they listened to the same movements of Wagner and the same operettas such as *Die Fledermaus* or *The Merry Widow*, they watched one or more films, always the same ones, they went to bed in the early hours or in the morning. The guide would recycle his monologues indefinitely, they were brain-numbing in their monotony. Monotone monologues: years passed, identical and serial.

Was it hypnotic? Work suffered, but they enjoyed themselves.

One lunchtime like all the others, in 1936 – though it could have been late 1933, during the honeymoon period of the guide and the young architect – Goebbels mentioned in passing that the head of the foreign press department had made fun of the

German volunteers in the Condor Legion in Spain and their lack of fighting spirit. Goebbels detested the head of the foreign press department, an old fellow traveller. He was one metre ninety-three, a giant, and his ironic nickname was 'Putzi', 'little one'. Goebbels was very small, with a club foot, ugly, all the old comrades agreed on that, they made fun of him, his club foot, his failed novels, his ugliness, and he hated Putzi.

The guide was scandalized by Putzi's comments as reported by Goebbels. How could anyone make fun of our boys? He, the guide, knew how they felt, he had seen action during the Great War, he had experienced fear and the courage required to overcome that fear.

The guide was scandalized, but at the same time saw a chance to play a joke.

Several identical, serial evenings went by in the Chancellery reception room. In the meantime, the joke played itself out, and on one of these identical, serial evenings Goebbels told them all about it. Hitler knew it by heart, but it was so funny that he liked hearing it again and again. Putzi had had to take a plane to Leipzig. When they were in the air, the pilot told him that he would in fact be set down in Spain, in 'red' territory, as it was known, where he would serve as a spy for Franco. It was an order from the Führer. Putzi panicked. He explained that it wasn't possible, that it must be a mistake, he wasn't prepared for it. He begged for hours, humiliated himself. The pilot was in on the joke, he was inflexible, kept giving him updates on the plane's progress, warned him to prepare for a forced landing.

The guide was in stitches at every stage of this story, his guests laughed along with him, the architect laughed. The plane had finally landed in Leipzig without incident. It was a good joke, Putzi had been taught a lesson. The circle of intimates were less amused when they learned that the head of the foreign press office, terrified by his adventure, had fled abroad, taking his secrets with him. In his memoirs, the architect was still laughing, no change of heart there, and he recounted a good number of such pranks, which the guide was very partial to and which he sometimes organized himself.

Another time, the butt of the joke was the house steward. He had done nothing wrong, he was a good, devoted servant. This was in the winter of 1939, it could have been in 1933, except that, no, it was wartime, and that provided some superb opportunities to construct jokes down to the minutest detail, like miniature battle plans.

In private, the guide informed him that he had been mobilized to join a rocket launcher unit. The steward was not a young man and he was horrified. For days he sought a way to bring the subject up with the guide, and the guide made the most of the situation, knowing that it would make his circle laugh, and enjoying the steward's clumsy attempts to approach him, to have a word in his ear. One day, the steward grasped the nettle, and the guide's response was a simple one. Alas, it was not possible to offer him special dispensation, the days of the 'System' were over, the shameful era of the Weimar Republic was finished, no more shirking at the taxpayers' expense. The steward was at his wits' end. He came up with a final argument: he would be of more use staying with him, as he was familiar with all his likes and dislikes, than in a *Nebelwerfer* unit.

The guide burst out laughing. The guide's little joke had succeeded just like his conquest of Poland had succeeded. He told the steward that it was just a joke.

They all laughed – the architect, Goebbels and all the others laughed as they listened to the guide. As the war progressed, the jokes stopped, and the laughs.

★

Goebbels would have liked to laugh at Speer's expense with the guide, and Bormann would have liked to laugh at Goebbels' and Speer's expense with the guide, but this wasn't possible. And when they saw the young architect and the Führer having one of their confabs over a drawing or a model, they understood that if Speer were to fall one day, the guide would never laugh at it, he would cry with rage, disappointment and rage, with tears of blood.

15

They made lots of trips to Munich to visit Professor Troost and to relive memories.

Munich, the guide would muse out loud in the train or on the plane on the way there, was not only a city that he had cherished since his early prewar years, when he had wanted to study at the Academy of Fine Arts after his bad experience in Vienna. Munich was a forge. Munich was the place where he had forged the signs of his genius. He knew he was a genius and destined for great things, and Munich was the place where he had found his voice for the first time in the bars in the evenings, when his audience would stop drinking to listen to him, suddenly fascinated by this teetotal vegetarian who detested male promiscuity with women and the use of prostitutes. The guide would bow extravagantly to women, use quite exaggerated expressions of politeness and admiration when women were introduced to him, and was not one much given to drinking and whoring – it wasn't his thing at all. But when he got up onto a table to speak, the bar would be filled with the air of another planet, and his voice transformed their shared frustration into a collective drive towards the radical happiness of Germany.

It was in Munich that he forged his facial style, that moustache, that hair parting, that stare, those hand and arm gestures that accompanied his voice. It was in Munich that he forged that voice that came from elsewhere and transmitted the air of another planet to his admirers. It was in Munich that he launched his war of signs – the voice, the facial expressions, the swastika he designed for the Party, the black uniforms – which soon the whole world would know, the newspapers of America, Britain, France, and which he wanted to amplify in stone, in gigantic monuments, a translation of his voice.

In the train or on the plane, the guide would suddenly start muttering diatribes, without raising that Munich-forged voice, diatribes in a voice as dull as a volcano rumbling just before it erupts, a slow, meticulous voice, expressing a unique, premeditated violence, a hatred that was beyond anger, a hatred based on diatribes against the Jews, against them in particular: the Jews.

The architect listened. He didn't feel strongly one way or the other about the Jews. He didn't really rub shoulders with any Jews, none of the professors he might have admired or detested was a Jew, and if he did know any, or claimed that he had known any, he showed them the same politeness that you would offer a stranger. But he wasn't obsessed with the Jews. Whether there were Jews there or not made not a whit of difference to his passion for mathematics and architecture, his ambitions, his plans for skiing trips or walks. Wherever he went, there was no welcoming Jewish innkeeper he would want to revisit nor any unwelcoming one he would despise. The Jews had never done anything to him, for good or ill, and whether they were there or not was a matter of complete indifference to him. If the guide was so obsessed with the Jews he must have his own reasons, no one is perfect, even if the architect might end up feeling bored and embarrassed by these sudden, vulgar harangues against the Jews that came out of nowhere.

The guide hated the Jews, but then he would suddenly think about Troost and start musing on what they would discover, the architect and him, at his studio, and he was excited, he loved Professor Troost, he hated the Jews, he loved Troost . . . he flitted from one subject to the other in a single sentence, dreaming out loud about the images he had in his head of this House of Art that he had commissioned from him. He pondered the possible layout of the ground floor. He pondered the porticos, which would have rectangular columns, rows of columns like giant soldiers standing to attention. He pondered the monumental dimensions of the site – 175 metres long, 75 metres wide, the guide remembered even the most minor measurements, because size mattered.

Size is fundamental; there is no obscene meaning to be found in this obsession with size.

The size of buildings had to exceed everything built in the past, since firstly it meant they were built to last and secondly it helped to subjugate the masses in the present. You just had to see the masses when they attended the cathedrals of that Jewish cult Christianity. You just had to see them subjugated by the vaults, the transepts, the enormous rose windows, subjugated by ritual and the vast scale of the space. You just had to see them subjugated by the cinema. Sleepwalkers.

The guide's war of signs encompassed the present day as well as the whole of history, the past as well as the future. With his gigantic buildings he would offer them rituals the likes of which they had never encountered, except in myths.

The architect never got bored of hearing this. He listened to the guide avidly and joined him in this still rather vague vision of gigantic buildings designed for new rituals.

They arrived at the railway station or airport in Munich, got in the car that was waiting for them – there were other cars behind and in front of them for the SS bodyguards – and the motorcade drove to a dilapidated courtyard in a street in Munich. It was the location of Professor Troost's studio, on the second floor of a building in the same sorry state as the courtyard, which made for a rather charming and authentically bohemian effect.

The guide felt quite at home there. Not without eloquence, he recalled that he had once been a bohemian artist himself, while vituperating against the Jewified officials who ran Viennese art in his younger days, when he had almost died of starvation. He implied that he hadn't chosen politics, it had chosen him while he was striving for the higher solitude of the bohemian artist. But Vienna and Munich belonged to the Jews and their Jewified friends. For now, he was simply honoured to have the chance to chat to artists and architects as in former times and to offer them his protection for their common projects while sharing their bohemian lifestyle, where everyone gets up late and goes to bed late.

Troost never met the guide at the foot of the stairs. The guide would go up, he was impatient, he couldn't 'wait a moment longer', he told him. In front of his young architect, he proclaimed: 'I couldn't wait a moment longer, Herr Professor, do you have anything new? Let's have a look!'

16

For months, the guide took the young architect to Munich on honeymoon.

They went once a fortnight or so, it was a honeymoon in bite-size instalments. They would have lunch or dinner at the Osteria Bavaria, the guide's favourite restaurant. They ate Italian food there – the guide was fond of ravioli. They went for walks. They hung around for a while, visiting Troost and other studios while dreaming of grand architectural and urban planning projects. They went to the villa of Heinrich Hoffmann, the guide's photographer. He always felt comfortable visiting the family of one of his oldest comrades, a pure Nazi, an art lover too, which was rare in the Party. Hoffmann was also an art publisher and seller. The guide loved being there, in their garden, lying on the lawn, sleeves rolled up, discoursing on the pictures that Hoffmann showed him. Oddly, he loved the paintings of Eduard von Grützner, who specialized in drunken, pot-bellied, red-headed monks imbibing various ambrosias. Vaguely reminiscent of Jordaens and Rubens perhaps. Did they remind the guide of the SA in the taverns of Munich? The architect was perplexed by this array of greasy hedonism and flesh collected by his sober, vegetarian guide. But the guide was like that, and at this stage his contradictions could be charming. He could surprise his friends as well as his enemies. It was at the Hoffmanns' one evening that he met a very young apprentice photographer.

He introduced himself to her as Herr Wolf, a play on his first name, Adolf, which means 'noble wolf'. Her name was Eva, but the guide never talked about her. He hid her. He belonged to the German people.

There were crowds. They were mostly unplanned. According to Speer's memoirs, these spontaneous outbursts of joy weren't staged. The guide would be recognized, a throng would gather around him, displaying a passion that was so much more than mere submission. The architect was fascinated. Of course, he was in thrall to the fact that, a few hours or even just a few minutes later, he would find himself in a restaurant or hotel bar in a one-to-one with this master who was adulated like a film star. This contrast bewitched him. Bewitched was the word he always used when pressed to explain his relationship with the guide. He would always answer their question with another question: who wouldn't be bewitched? Who wasn't?

The young architect considered these trips to Munich as a turning point in his career. He reckoned that the guide wanted Troost to pass on his knowledge to him, to establish a line of filiation. Preoccupied as he was with time running out, with the limited number of years he had to realize his projects – that was his current refrain, 'the few years that I have left' – the guide must surely have wanted to ensure the future of the monuments initiated by Troost by putting the young architect under his tutelage. That must have been the reason.

The young architect imagined a master–disciple relationship with Troost, much the same as the one he had had with Tessenow. He was already relishing the prospect of working in his shadow.

And then, on 21 January 1934, Troost died unexpectedly of pneumonia.

On that day, the young architect was in a waiting room at the Ministry of Propaganda. A subordinate of Goebbels was congratulating him. He shared his master's frame of mind, cynicism dressed up as humour, and he often laughed at his own cynicism to provoke laughter in his audience. He smoked cigars, he had a round head, he was debonair, with a vulgar mouth and jowly cheeks, and he said to the young architect: 'Congratulations, Speer! From now on you're number one!'

A Perfect Match

(1934–1939)

17

A large pool of dried blood stained the floor of a palace in Berlin. The young architect felt nothing except disgust which made him turn on his leather-booted heels. He was carrying out his umpteenth refit, preparing for the transfer of the headquarters of the Munich SA to the Reich capital. It was definitely to be the last. The monumental projects that had been dreamed up on paper were finally starting to happen.

The guide's repetitive evenings had been enlivened by some good news. He had just crushed an attempted putsch by his former best friend Ernst Röhm, the founder and head of the Sturmabteilung, the SA. The SA had been indispensable before they had taken over power, in the deadly brawls with the communists; it became a danger when it set out to replace the official army with a popular army. The SA had been quietly opposed to the new links that the guide had forged with the traditional bourgeoisie. Its chiefs had been preparing a revolution with financial support from France. At least, that was the official line, and the young architect did not delve too deeply. The guide himself had gone, revolver in hand, to oversee the arrest of Röhm and his staff at Bad Wiessee, next to Lake Tegern in Bavaria. It was a pretty, typically German village, unfortunately sullied by the frequent visits of Röhm and his crew.

The guide described what he saw as he went from room to

room with his gun to personally arrest this scum: mature men in couples and totally naked young men in couples. There was no doubt about what they had been doing together all night. And these were not isolated cases. There were almost three million members of the SA: what if homosexuality was widespread throughout the whole organization? What if it was infiltrating the whole of Germany because of these degenerates and their French backers?

The inner circle all guffawed and sneered, they became indignant and angry, they insisted that the SA was steeped in an atmosphere of homosexual debauchery, at least among the general staff, with their base predilection for barbecue, beer and cross-dressing.

The young architect listened casually. He was a prince. He was twenty-nine years old. His tall frame was often dressed in an elegant double-breasted suit which accentuated his slim figure, and he listened to the 45-year-old guide telling stories about mature men and naked young men in bedrooms on the shores of Lake Tegern in Bavaria. He was not especially perturbed. He was basking in the dream come true of his success with one of the most powerful men on earth. He spoke to him only of architecture, art, urban planning; he was above all this, politics didn't interest him, he made sure that the oafish members of the inner circle believed that politics didn't interest him. And they did see him a bit like one of those women who were occasionally granted admission to their circle. They never discussed politics, they weren't allowed to, the guide hated hearing them venture onto such topics and was consternated on their behalf if they ever did. In his view, women and artists shouldn't be preoccupied with politics, only with beauty. For different reasons, of course: women should be beautiful like movie actresses, artists should produce beauty, but women and artists somehow both inhabited the plane of beauty. The young architect was no exception to this and he combined the two: his physical beauty and the beauty of his sketches on paper.

In front of witnesses, the guide soon demanded that he wear the uniform of the Party. In private, the guide preferred to wear civilian clothes, but in public the burden of Nazi power was such that, alas – the guide expressed some strange regrets sometimes – one had to wear boots and the whole glorious military kit when out among the crowds and the masses. The guide liked grumbling about the things he himself imposed. It was a vanity that many of his collaborators aped: complaining about the things they themselves had ordered. They would do it incessantly. Especially Himmler. Complain about the onerous duty of waging war on the Jews across the whole of conquered Europe. Complain about the onerous duty of murdering Jewish women and children. Complain about not having done it well enough and disappointing the Führer. Complain about not spending enough time with his own wife and his own kids, with their pretty little blond heads.

Did the architect complain that he was seeing less and less of his wife? Later, he would claim that he complained about it from the very start of his relationship with the guide.

The architect never spoke to the guide about his wife. From then on, he wore a uniform, with the rank of head of division under Rudolf Hess. Later it would be Goebbels. He would have preferred Göring. He had always had a soft spot for Göring, who was easier to handle, more addicted to his pleasures and so weaker. But these assignments were merely nominal. He really reported to only one man, the guide. It was a relationship with no intermediary. This uniform was his wedding suit.

18

One day, one of his associates, a certain Karl Maria Hettlage, said out loud what everyone had been thinking with a mixture of stupor, amusement and jealousy. Hettlage was an SS officer, a lawyer responsible for expelling the Jews out of Berlin to make space for the building of future monuments. They had just been inspecting the models for the umpteenth time. He had observed how the Führer looked at the architect and listened to him.

So, on the way out, he said to him: 'Do you know who you are, Speer? You are Hitler's unrequited love.'

Or perhaps he said: 'You are our Führer's unrequited love.'

He was in the SS, this was just before the war or right at the beginning, a time of Nazi victories, and Hitler's name wasn't bandied about like that. He almost certainly used the title 'Führer'.

Or maybe he never made this comment at all.

Hettlage is a novel unto himself, like his master Speer. A brilliant lawyer, a brilliant technocrat, he would survive the war and become secretary of state for finances in the Federal Republic of Germany under Adenauer, then a member of the High Authority of the European Coal and Steel Community, then once again secretary of state of the Federal Finance Ministry. He would exemplify one of those sinister ironies much prized by the members of Hitler's inner circle: having participated in the Nazi regime's expulsion of Jews from Berlin, which meant their death, he would, as part of his postwar duties, oversee compensation for the victims of medical experiments in the concentration camps.

In 1939 or 1940, is it possible that he could without fear, without embarrassment, in such a familiar fashion, have hinted at a homosexual attraction between Hitler and Speer, in front of the very person concerned? Historians seem not to have asked him about this. He has never confirmed or denied having made the remark. True or false, it is a brilliantly snide comment, worthy of a Berlin cabaret show in one of Luchino Visconti's later films.

'You are the Führer's unrequited love . . .'

The architect was taken aback, his usual sangfroid suddenly undermined. What did he mean by that? But Hettlage didn't retract, nor did he display any fear that he had said too much – that fear of speaking out that was so common in Germany from the top to the bottom of the Nazi regime. After all, he was SS, and Speer, his boss, wasn't. And he continued, with a mysterious hint of warning: 'For better or worse, remember!' The marriage vow.

19

Nuremberg, 1934

An alleyway of granite several kilometres long crossed an esplanade covering several hectares. It was a stage, a void, a paean to emptiness, or else its diversion, its perversion. On this stage, blocks of people gathered in groups, broke up, formed into rows and squares, like on a chessboard.

It was the annual congress of the NSDAP in Nuremberg, its first monumental edition, with all the attendant trappings. Totally different from the previous year. What was previously wood had now been set in stone.

Along each side, horizontal lines stretched almost to infinity, bleachers, the stairs that accessed them, bleachers that themselves seemed like stairs, a series of parallel lines converging to a vanishing point, a paean to the line, or rather its diversion, its perversion.

Everywhere flags, swastika banners. A debauchery of fabrics printed with swastikas flapping in the wind across the whole city. And here, above the stands, the flags, the banners were enormous.

The entrance was not really an entrance, two porticos, one esplanade, a memorial to the dead of the First World War.

At the opposite end of the esplanade, something resembling an altar.

Was it an altar?

The foreign visitors – ambassadors, journalists, sundry VIPs – who were attending the National Socialist ritual at Nuremberg for the first time, wondered whether it actually was an altar.

There too, there were bleachers, and steps giving access to the bleachers, horizontal, parallel lines, mounting an assault on the sky.

It was certainly a rostrum, the visitors knew that much. That was its function, to be a rostrum of honour, one where the guide and the potentates of the regime would have to stand and face the chessboard spread out before them, with its rows and squares which were in fact blocks of people. It measured several hundred metres long, several dozen metres high – the architect, but more particularly the guide, when he visited the site, gave the precise measurements, he knew them by heart: 390 metres long, 24 metres high. It was surmounted by columns. At each end, boxing in the tiny human pawns sitting on the lines of the bleachers, were two enormous plinths. They were like the supports for some missing lighthouse of Alexandria.

In the centre, cutting across the lines, massive cuboids piled one on top of the other. It was the stage itself, where the guide would speak. Above his head was an enormous swastika circled by a crown of oak leaves.

On this stone outcrop, this terrace worthy of a palace, the guide really felt like the guide, the Führer. And everyone could feel it too.

When he addressed the blocks of people spread out before him, in their chessboard rows and squares, he hypnotized them, the pedestal from which he spoke was worthy of the voice he had honed in Munich, and there, more than ever, he was really the Führer – the guide.

The foreign visitors had their answer: it was an altar more than a rostrum. It was as brutally simple as that. That's what the architect had intended. An imitation, an absurd descendant of the great altar of Pergamon, one of the seven wonders of the ancient world, reproduced in the eponymous museum in Berlin. In the previous century, a German archaeologist had discovered the ruins of the altar in Greece. He had transported them back to Germany and restored and reinvented the altar. It signified that it was a German, and not a Frenchman or an Englishman, who had rediscovered this heap of ruins. Since then, generations of young architects had flocked in to study the result, which was basically a load of kitsch.

Such remarks about kitsch no longer bothered the young architect. The good taste he had acquired as an adolescent and throughout his studies alongside Tessenow was no longer the order of the day in Germany. In fact, the National Socialists had their own concept of kitsch, which they abhorred. They abhorred the sick art of their century: cubism, dadaism, surrealism, Soviet constructivism, all kitsch, all contaminated by Jews and the Jewified. National Socialists wore boots, goose-stepped, gave Roman salutes at the slightest pretext, some of their chiefs such as Göring wore ostentatious costumes, they waxed grandiloquent. Foreign ambassadors and journalists, in their notes or articles, described them as cowards in suits and vulgar kitsch dummies; foreign ambassadors and journalists declared that they had created a whole politics of kitsch; but none of this mattered. The National Socialists declared war on kitsch and on taste, whether good or bad. Questions of taste were bourgeois, and National Socialism saw itself as anti-bourgeois.

Preparing the rally, poring over his drawing board, in trains, planes and the Mercedes that took him all over the Reich in the wake of the guide, the young architect had been thinking about his own past, his restricted upbringing, and how his future had been mapped out by his family.

He was born into the well-off bourgeoisie of old Germany, a cultivated milieu in which the architecture bequeathed from father to son was but one among many doors of the arts and sciences – he loved mathematics and would have loved to become a mathematician, to open the door of mathematics. These doors opened into a relatively harmonious room, society itself, which was essentially liberal in nature, a place where ideas were debated, criticized, where the bourgeoisie itself was criticized, debated as a class, often by sons in conflict with fathers, and even in recent times some daughters. But he knew that the bourgeoisie he came from would never have conceived of the 'Field for the Reich Party Congress', the name given to the Nuremberg complex he was in the process of building, of which the Zeppelin field, a homage to the airships floating constantly overhead, was just one element among many. It would never have dared, for fear of offending good taste and provoking sneers and waspish comments about this massive edifice.

He knew that his architecture was violating all the conventions of taste and the language of forms and was surprised by how he took pleasure from it. It was to the guide that he owed this pleasure. It was to him that he owed his liberation from these old restrictions. What architect would not want that? To build freed from the strictures of taste and with money no object?

It was much more than a mere reprise of Antiquity, more than the latest revivalism, where pediments, peristyles, cornices, Corinthian or Ionian columns can sometimes be seen, more than another of those neoclassical waves that have recurred since the Renaissance, producing excellent architecture from Rome to St Petersburg, from Berlin to the whole of Italy, then Vienna and of course Paris – the Arc de Triomphe, the Opéra Garnier.

To the guide's autodidactic mind, the boundaries between genres were fluid, and he was quite able to conflate the neoclassical with the baroque. These terms had no meaning any more, and the young, cultivated, highly qualified architect had no problem accepting this corruption of judgement and of genres; he adapted to it, found it liberating, building without concern for cost or for reason and blowing the budget as if he were directing a blockbuster.

When he showed his father what he was working on, his father examined it carefully and in the end said just one sentence: 'You've gone mad.'

Like all styles of architecture, his used stone and mortar, but more than the others, it used flesh. It used human flesh as much as stone and mortar – human pawns in the hands of a mad geometer, of an abstract art not so far away from those paintings the Nazis hated so much, like brown Mondrians. And to these building blocks it added cosmology.

20

It added the night.

It was night, and the night was an integral part of the construction.

The architecture of the Zeppelin field employed granite, marble, the flesh of human pawns, but the first time the architect saw all this flesh, these hundreds of thousands of human pawns assembled at the rehearsals, he found it rather ugly. The flesh was largely fat, belts were strained to breaking, mouths oozed greasy saliva and oily breath. The members of the Party had grown fat after less than one year in power. Pig, pork sausages and shanks, beer, spirits, all the antisemitic diatribes, all the crude abuses of the Jews created an ugliness that the brown webbed uniforms struggled to conceal.

The guide agreed. The architect was right. All this fat had to be sublimated, this gross heap of human pawns orchestrated into his ritual.

So the architect suggested parading all the functionaries at night. In the darkness, their decadent anatomies would not be noticeable. At night you can control ugliness through lighting. What you illuminate, what you don't illuminate.

The architect – the artist – would make night the essential building material of the Zeppelin field. Stone was nothing more than a structure to support the night. A foundation, nothing more. The night was the true building, and the stands, the columns and the esplanade were merely the foundations, the basement. It was perhaps the first time that night had been made solid like this.

The architect had a brainwave. It was brutal but beautiful, he was sure of that. He had seen Göring's new anti-aircraft searchlights. Their beams cast strange, immaterial, dazzling columns kilometres into the sky with no loss of intensity. These beams were like the ghosts of ancient columns.

He convinced the guide, who convinced Göring to lend them to him.

He placed 130 of them along the four stone stands.

The effect exceeded all expectations. There were clouds on the first night of the rally, and the columns of light rose up to hit them, illuminating them; it looked like a ceiling painted as a sky. The cosmos and the weather were the backdrop for the guide's speech on Germany's rediscovered greatness. At certain moments, the searchlights tilted and criss-crossed, forming a dome of light like nothing ever seen before.

The architect saw it as the supreme expression of his romantic aspirations. A translation of German romanticism itself. And this time the visitors concurred. 'A dome of light', a 'cathedral of ice' were some of the comments made by enraptured foreign journalists, writers and ambassadors.

As for the members of the inner circle, they were stupefied. This spectacle was a declaration of love for the Führer.

The darkness, the searchlights, the light on him when he appeared and quietly began his speech – as if he were speaking in everyone's ear, regardful of their frustration, of how they had suffered as Germans, as soldiers, workers and unemployed

Germans tricked by the 'System', of the right as well as the left, before uniting them all into a single vengeful mass by his vengeful voice against the foreign powers and the Jews – this whole performance enhanced the standing of the guide as never before, and the standing of the architect in the eyes of the guide. They were dancing a waltz together.

Most of the members of the circle were soldiers, paramilitaries or police. Even Goebbels the failed writer was one. They had realized too late how hugely important architecture was to the guide. They had held on to the belief that his aborted vocation was nothing more than a sad memory of his youth which had been largely compensated for by political passion. They had convinced themselves that the guide's sudden infatuation for the young architect was merely the product of some passing nostalgia.

They were wrong. The two went hand in hand: architectural plan and battle plan.

The man of power wanted to be an architect, but that wasn't the end of it. The architect equally wanted to be a man of power.

The vast resources granted to the young architect gave him an exhilarating feeling of power. The inner circle could all see this: he became brittle and authoritarian. Himmler headed the army of the SS, Göring headed the Luftwaffe, Speer started small with a tiny regiment of specialized workers. For now, that was enough. It was up to him to surpass the past masters. The guide would perhaps surpass Alexander and certainly Frederick II of Prussia; Speer would perhaps surpass Praxiteles and certainly Karl Friedrich Schinkel, the architect of Frederick II of Prussia.

But this was just a first step towards a more insidious ambition.

At Nuremberg he had not just built a monument. The stone, the human flesh, the night, the light of anti-aircraft searchlights created a spectacle of unlimited ambition. It was the politicization of aesthetics and the aestheticization of politics.

It was something that the military and paramilitaries in the Party, despite their innate sense of violence, did not see coming. Except for fat Bormann. Martin Bormann, the Führer's lackey, the biggest oaf of them all, who grabbed the secretaries' behinds, and was obsequious with everyone while bad-mouthing them before the guide, was in fact the most clear-sighted when it came to Speer. He was suspicious of him from the start. That haughty shyness, that remote diffidence, that handsome face and apparent indifference to politics, supposedly harmless despite him being the Führer's favourite, these were all bluffs.

Goebbels should have spotted it, mused Bormann, since he fancied himself as a writer: art is the fruit of an excessive ambition. Art is the opposite of humility, of the public good, of good itself, and of evil for that matter. Art competes with God, if he exists. Art attacks death, it's as simple as that. Stone lasts longer than flesh, it's as simple as that. These are truisms, the expression of a brutal, banal, irrefutable common sense. They express the basic truth of stone: carved by human flesh, it lasts longer than that flesh. The pyramids remain; the qualified workers who built them remain with them, even if their names haven't survived. Even slaves remain in some way, when they work on raising the buildings of art.

The Führer didn't want just to conquer space, he wanted to conquer time. What use are conquests without commemorative monuments? What use is space without time?

This was what the guide was for the architect, the rest didn't matter, it was of secondary importance – his hatred of the Jews, for example. The architect and the guide completed each other very well.

And then everyone could see it – the VIP foreigners, the VIPs of National Socialism: in his staging of Nuremberg, he was not different from the potentates of the regime. He was one of them.

What Göring was to costume – all those uniforms laden with ermine, breastplates and medals – Speer was to architecture – the plethora of flags, columns, searchlights. What was ridiculous at the level of the individual – Göring and his outfits – was equally so at the level of the collective, but it was more abstract, more spectacular, more dangerous. Speer knew this very well. Speer's father knew this and it saddened him. Speer's old mentor, Tessenow, knew it too and said to him one day: 'Do you think you are making something that will last? It makes an impression, that's all.'

He knew it, the inner circle knew it, he was creating pomp and pageantry way beyond mere architectural necessity. He was a politician. He was a potential Göring.

21

A woman – an actress, a director – pulled out an old press clipping from 1931. Only three years earlier, but it was already another world. The article was about the refurbishment of the House of the Party carried out by the young architect at that time. The woman explained that, although she didn't know him at the time, she couldn't resist cutting out his face.

When the young architect asked her why, she told him that, with a face like that, she thought one day he might play a role . . .

She left the sentence hanging in the air, before finishing:

'Play a role in one of my films, of course.'

Anyone who happened to be there would have seen this as a classic attempt at seduction. The young architect was flattered because this beautiful actress had noticed his pretty face. He had just been told how handsome he was.

The film director was called Leni Riefenstahl. She had filmed the Party Congress at Nuremberg that Speer had just mounted. It was the mise en scène of a mise en scène. It was an avant-garde notion where you would least expect it, a representation of a representation.

Some foreign spectators agreed: in the murky depths of the new Germany, two very talented artists stood out. Leni Riefenstahl and Albert Speer were young, beautiful and talented, and the Führer loved them. But around them and their Führer there was a court of mediocre, ugly cretins. In particular there was Goebbels, who loved screwing actresses and had attempted to rape Riefenstahl. There was Martin Bormann, who pestered the pretty secretaries at the Chancellery and wanted to block Speer's rise by favouring other architects before the Führer and by bogging down his plans with administrative obstacles, which annoyed Speer and left him feeling humiliated for a long time afterwards.

They were young, beautiful and talented, and the attempted rape suffered by Riefenstahl and the vexations visited upon Speer might have brought them together. They might have flirted. They might have had a love affair. She would have been up for it. She had already shown that. They might have consoled each other over the attempted rape and the vexations. They might have helped each other out with their respective artistic endeavours, inspired each other. Of course, there would have been feelings of rivalry. Of course, love affairs between artists are eaten away from within by jealousy and rivalry. Even love affairs between artists and men of power are eaten away from within by the ambition of the former and the paranoia of the latter, the poisonous questioning of the true meaning of this professional love. Am I ever loved for reasons solely to do with love? Am I ever loved like characters in films are loved, in those scenes that the director knew so well, and which the Führer and his inner circle enjoyed watching in the evening, after a dinner ponderous with repetitive conversations? Was the Führer really loved by Germany? The Germans seemed to love him. And he himself declared that he loved only Germany.

Be this as it may, the young director and the young architect would certainly have understood each other. They shared a culture that far surpassed that of the hapless oafs of the guide's entourage. They even appreciated new artists that the guide did not appreciate.

They might have talked more and more openly with each other. They might eventually have become more aware. They might eventually have thought about escaping. They might have fled like other artists they knew, especially her, as she knew many more than him.

It would have been a German love story with a hint of Hollywood.

It would have been a plausible scenario, given how the director showed her intention by handing him the photo of his face that she had cut out of the newspaper. This meeting at the height of their success; this still strange, seductively unhealthy backdrop against which they met; this baroque militarized police-state of the Third Reich that they themselves had built over and above the expectations of their patron Adolf Hitler, with these columns of stone and light, the ubiquitous banners, the camera movements, the high- and low-angle shots, the contrasts, the perspectives, the striking montages; the ever-stronger bonds formed between the people of power at the heart of this world; the attempted rapes, the vexations they encountered despite their success, bringing home to them how fragile their position was; the stolen, secret conversations after lovemaking in an anonymous room, because the rooms of the Reich's palaces, the Hotel Adlon for example, were bugged; the passionate conversations on art and politics; the passionate scenes of love because they were young, beautiful and dear to the Führer and because they were so passionate about politics and art; pillow talk of those who had already left, artists they knew and whose work they admired; those who left and those who stayed; their subsequent awareness and their flight . . .

This would seem to be how the scenario should play out from the moment the director first made those flattering remarks to the architect.

22

But it didn't even cross their minds.

Did they simply, each in their solitary work as official artists, harbour the unspoken thought of fleeing the Reich without discussing it with each other?

They knew lots of artists, especially her, Leni Riefenstahl. She personally knew everyone in the film world, she had Jewish friends and lovers, sexy young Jewish cameramen, elegant, slim, older Jewish producers. She wasn't repelled by men, she liked filming young, handsome soldiers, athletes. The guide's immediate entourage was made up of ugly boors with unhealthy lifestyles at the opposite end of the scale to the cult of the body and sport she found in the Hitler Youth and the SS, when they marched past in shorts or donned their swimming costumes to tackle the cold water of Germany's romantic lakes and rivers. Apart from a few exceptions, there was only the architect Speer, at twenty-nine, who was neither boorish nor ugly.

Some of her Jewish friends and lovers had left. Like Harry Sokal, her Jewish lover and producer. She had tried to get him to read *Mein Kampf*, the guide's bestseller, but he shrugged his shoulders at his talented, ambitious and stupid German mistress of Aryan stock and went elsewhere, France probably, she didn't know and didn't give it much thought. Even her rival and friend Marlene Dietrich, who had pinched the lead role in *The Blue Angel* by the great Josef von Sternberg (a Viennese Jew) from under her nose, had stayed in America and refused Goebbels' persistent demands to return to the new Reich, where a pot of gold awaited her.

Why should she leave? She wasn't Jewish. She was a German citizen of Aryan stock, according to the new protocol where you had to prove your race, and she wasn't interested in politics. She wasn't Jewish like slim, elegant, unhappy Harry, the archetypal Germanic, sophisticated Berliner. She wasn't just a simple actress, like Marlene. She was a director. She had more strings to her bow than Marlene, and she wasn't Jewish like Harry. The Nazi Party commissioned her to make films, and she could have access to whatever she needed. Who would say no to that? Who would leave?

The young architect also knew some artists. True, he didn't know any German Jewish artists, except by name, but he personally knew some non-Jewish German artists who weren't members of the NSDAP. Also some who were members of the Party. He liked the architects of the Bauhaus, which the guide despised and which the inner circle despised even more because the guide despised it so much. He especially liked the artists that the guide liked, the sculptors Arno Breker and Josef Thorak. They sculpted naked muscular men and naked muscular women that the guide appreciated, monumental, martial figures, with the furious, pathetic constipated expression you must have at the thought of being naked for eternity in front of crowds of people you don't know.

One evening, the guide, the young architect, the Gauleiter of Bavaria and a few others were dining in Munich. It was a relaxed atmosphere at the Osteria Bavaria, and they were there for the launch of the annual exhibition of German art that was taking place at the House of Art designed by Paul Troost. They endlessly discussed the same painters and the same sculptors. Suddenly, the gauleiter from Bavaria declared that Josef Thorak was not fit to put up statues in the Reich. He had recently signed a communist proclamation. Whether it was actually communist in the accepted sense of the term or whether the gauleiter had interpreted a simple artist's protest against some Nazi directive to do with art, no one thought to ask. Everyone remained silent. Josef Thorak was the sculptor most favoured by the young architect, and he stayed silent before this sudden attack of which he was indirectly the target.

But the guide knew artists better than they knew themselves. He had been an artist himself, unlike the gauleiter and many of his old Munich comrades, those beer-bellied SA members. They were indispensable against the Jews, but they didn't understand the German artists of Aryan stock favoured by the guide. The guide was in a mellow mood that evening in Munich, he felt at home in the bohemian ambience of bars and studios that reminded him of his younger days as a painter. 'You know,' he said, 'I don't attach a great deal of importance to that. You should never judge artists by their political views. Their imagination, which they need for their work, prevents them from thinking in realistic terms. Let Thorak work for us. Artists are pure innocents. One day, they sign a petition with their eyes closed; the next day, they sign another, as long as they feel it's for a good cause.'

23

Who would want to leave after hearing that, thought the architect, who recounted these remarks by Hitler in his memoirs. The ones who left did so because they had no choice. They were Jews – it was sad that they had to leave, but art goes on and life goes on, especially when one is in the service of the great art championed by the guide in his monumental projects.

The years went by, the congresses went by, orders increased, the architect's life was delicious, his stress increased, his guts paid the price, the years went by, delicious and stressful, full of passionate tensions within the inner circle, with everyone exercising greater, more autonomous power, and coming into conflict with each other, in an environment where the guide did little work, where the guide signed off virtually nothing, the Führer's orders were just hateful or honeyed words pronounced a cappella, and the members of the circle vied with each other and sought ever more ingenious ways to enact the desires the guide had expressed in Berlin, Munich or in the mountains, in his beloved Berghof.

1938. The architect spent a day inspecting the charred remains of the grand synagogue in Berlin, which had been burned down the previous night. He said that he felt a deep embarrassment at all the disorder, but would not admit to any other emotion.

He was very bourgeois, he knew this and made no bones about it in his memoirs. He was very good at self-criticism and giving the impression that he sat in judgement on himself and even to some extent found himself guilty. For him, with his bourgeois sensibility, there were things that you just didn't do: all this debris on full view in the capital, all this suffering open to the heavens, all these very unromantic ruins. Disorder was an abomination. Goebbels was abominable for the terrible way he had organized this Reich-wide pogrom.

Still, he couldn't do anything without losing all respect from a man he loved. And since he had had no part in these abuses, he felt blameless. He was simply the guide's favourite architect, no more nor less.

And if people were as honest as they claimed to be at great length in the anti-fascist forums in the Soviet Union, France, Britain and elsewhere, they couldn't deny his innocence. If the guide himself recognized the political innocence of artists, the democrats in Paris, Washington and London must surely be able to do likewise if they were sincerely free and sincerely passionate about art. He was innocent, he was an artist, he hadn't done anything wrong, and no one could blame him for having erected monuments in the Third Reich on a scale to match that of former civilizations, larger, even, in terms of volume, the sheer number of cubic metres and square metres, where one breathed the air of a different planet.

In fact, he was rewarded as Leni Riefenstahl was rewarded. The filmmaker won the grand prize for cinema at the Universal Exposition in Paris in 1937 for one of her films on the Party Congress at Nuremberg. The architect won the gold medal for architecture at the same exhibition. He had designed a tall building, punctuated by pilasters, with no other function than to support a gigantic eagle holding a swastika ringed by oak leaves in its claws. It was architecture celebrating power that celebrated architecture. Why the pilasters, if not to make 'architecture'? Why these cornices, these grooves, these labyrinth motifs incised in the walls between the pilasters, if not for the same reason? It made the average person think. It made them think on an epic scale. It made them think of the watercolour illustrations of ancient temples in their school books. It made them think of a Greece for all ages, a thousand-year-old architecture.

The artist designed it in response to the Soviet building, the model for which he is said to have discovered on an unannounced visit to the Paris International Exposition a few weeks previously. Through some mischief on the part of the organizers or pure chance, the Nazi pavilion faced the Soviet one on the right bank of the Seine, between the Eiffel Tower and the Palais de Chaillot. They stood either side of the open space in front of the Pont d'Iéna, in the city the guide considered to be the most beautiful in the world, even though he had never visited it. The whole world was amazed at the Soviet and Nazi pavilions facing each other in Paris, like two towers simultaneously watching and blocking each other.

The architect won the gold medal, but so did the Soviets. It was the first false note of history. Nazis and Soviets ending their duel level-pegging. In chess it is known as a stalemate.

24

The members of the circle were ecstatic. They were sure that Speer had just committed a terrible blunder.

He had presented the Führer with a drawing of some old-fashioned ruins, like something from the eighteenth century, showing his own construction of the Zeppelin field in Nuremberg overrun by ivy, some parts crumbling to the ground, the stones piled up one on top of the other like lovers' bodies. The stands were riddled with huge cracks, nature overgrowing them and smothering them in its vegetal embrace.

It was the future of the new Germany, the ruins of the 'thousand-year Reich', all those monuments that the guide had wanted to be immortal.

The expression 'the thousand-year Reich' was cropping up everywhere now, in the newspapers and in the speeches of the Party chiefs. No one can remember who came up with the phrase. Did the guide coin it in one of his speeches, or was it Goebbels in similar fashion? Or did it first appear in one of those repetitive conversations at the Chancellery or the Osteria Bavaria in Munich or at Berchtesgaden? Or was it the work of a Nazi journalist? The foreign press picked up on it and either made fun of it, fretted about it or got excited about it, if they saw it as the only project of civilization capable of thwarting communist barbarism – there were rumours of organized famine in Ukraine, with millions dead and acts of cannibalism.

The British talked about their empire 'where the sun never set'. Meanwhile the Germans of Aryan stock were the 'thousand-year Reich'.

Time counters space. Even if the Jew Albert Einstein had declared that the two were inseparable, National Socialism knew that time would crush space with the massive grace of its domes, its triumphal arches, its porticos, its stadiums of whatever type.

Space-time was just an elucubration of Jewish scientists, but the truth was more magical than that, according to certain theories in vogue among the SS. For them, the Earth was hollow, or else the Earth was a ball suspended in a cave, and what we took for stars were just the glittering walls of this cave. And there was still the idea that the Universe was just a clash of ice and fire, an elemental conflict, the mastery of which would lead to victory. Himmler loved that; he financed a vast amount of research and had especially high hopes for archaeology. He wanted to prove that the Germanic people were at the origin of the civilized world, that they inspired the Egyptians, the Greeks, the Romans, the Incas, the Chinese, the Japanese. So he had the earth of the Fatherland scraped for the slightest Germanic artefact, he invited the press whenever a piece of flint or pottery was extracted from the German mud, he was in raptures about the near-ubiquity of the swastika on the planet. These objects that the SS presented to the world were rather pathetic, common, everyone agreed, but Himmler was so happy, no one could bring themselves to pour cold water on his enthusiasm.

The guide took offence at this and mocked him in front of his intimate circle, as the architect took great delight in remembering when he came to write his memoirs around 1967. It is true that from 1942 onwards the Reichsführer-SS became one of his worst enemies, and memories are weapons, especially when the person concerned is dead.

So the guide was sad to see Himmler behave in this way. 'Why remind the whole world that we don't have a past? It is not enough that the Romans were already great builders when our ancestors lived in mud huts, Himmler has to start digging up these mud villages and get carried away at every piece of terracotta and every stone axe . . . The only thing that proves is that we were waving stone axes around and huddling round campfires when Greece and Rome were already at their cultural peak. Instead of keeping silent, Himmler makes a big hoopla about it! How the Romans of old would have laughed at these revelations! And that myth of the SS, how absurd is that? We reach a stage when we are virtually free of mysticism, and then it all starts up again! We might as well have stuck with the Church. At least it had traditions. To think that one day they might make me into an SS saint! I would be spinning in my grave!'

Speer laughed, the inner circle all laughed at Himmler kicking over the soil of German excavations in his black jackboots.

Shortly after the Congress, the young architect passed by the steel debris of a modern hangar that had been demolished to make way for the new complex. He was struck by how ugly the rusting steel beams were, struck by the ugliness of the ruins of all this modern architecture, built out of vulgar materials, devoid of any perceptible finishing, without any ornamentation. His mind was set alight. The guide's dismissal of Himmler's archaeological whims, the ugliness of modern buildings, even uglier when dismantled, his knowledge of romanticism, his knowledge of paintings of ancient ruins so prized by the romantics, his knowledge of the guide's tendency to fall into romantic languor when faced with ruined acropolises . . . all of this converged in a single intuition.

The present-day grandeur of Germany lay in the future ruins that would be uncovered, not in the crude remains that were vaunted by Himmler.

Contemporary buildings should be built with a mind to the ruins that they would later become. It was already an architecture of impact because of its outsize dimensions. It would be even more so if they could prefigure now what sort of ruin it would produce.
 It wasn't just a case of using the most durable and most noble materials – the best stones, the best wood, the best fabrics – in the service of durable and noble forms – domes, colonnades – but of using engineering and physics to predict the spots where the cracks would be most beautiful, where the disintegration would be most eloquent and full of pathos.

When the artist brought along his drawings illustrating the ruins of his Nuremberg, he shrugged off the indignation of the inner circle. They really were a bunch of cretins: scandalized that the thousand-year Reich could be shown in such a state and at the thought of its disappearance. Yes, one day the Reich would disappear, but its final victory would be in its ruins.

He presented his intuition to the guide. He called it *Theory of Ruin Value*. He apologized for the pretentiousness and pomposity of the title. He was adept at self-criticism as and when needed. He was adept at anticipating any criticism and building it into his argument in order to defuse it.

★

The guide was blown away.

He had always been fascinated by the fallen beauty of the past. By destruction. Destroying was as important as constructing, to leave a trace that will live in people's memory for ever. An aesthetics of destruction was a major innovation that not even Michelangelo or Praxiteles could have come up with.

From now on, the guide ordained, every large building designed in Germany must satisfy the theory of ruin value.

They had known each other for a few years now. They were in total agreement on all subjects – construction, destruction, ruins. The members of the circle all had immense power in their respective domains and now they tried to outdo one another to satisfy the Führer's orders concerning construction, destruction and ruins. Whether in armaments, the Jews, the economy, information and disinformation, they were all acting on their own initiative.

The young architect wanted to believe that he had achieved something in the field of the history of architecture. He now believed that his name was indissociable from this history, with his dome of light and his theory of ruin value.

In a way, it was already over, he thought with a touch of romantic nostalgia. The guide thought the same. The guide lamented his poor health incessantly, the very few years he had left to see all his projects with Speer rise from the ground. What they would do next, he would think in the middle of the night after the mind-numbing viewings of mind-numbing comedies and westerns, would be nothing more than amplification and repetition. It had all been said, even if they would not hesitate to resay it and redo it – the guide loved the Wagnerian repetition and amplification of a unique, obsessional theme – by premeditating more and more monumental children across the whole of Germany. In Nuremberg, emptied after each congress of its masses of human flesh, of its columns of light and its gigantic swastika banners, the silent esplanade and the innumerable lines of bleachers and stairs whipped by the wind already had an air of ruin about them.

Offspring

(One Thousand Years)

25

An ordinary Nazi reception in the prewar Reich. The guide walked among the couples, greeting the women like a pimple-faced young boy, judging the husbands. He was exaggeratedly, ridiculously courteous. A middle-school student awkwardly bowing and making absurd compliments like a character in an operetta, they all thought to themselves. Those who survived would say it out loud, later, after the defeat, when the Führer's sexuality would become the object of intense comic conjecture about the size of his penis, the number of his testicles, or his supposed hermaphrodite frigidity. Even the young architect would say it.

The men thought this, but the women thought something very different. The wives of the members of the inner circle, the female celebrities that were sometimes invited, the secretaries and cooks in his retinue did not think at all the same way as the men. They found the Führer charming, respectful and reassuring, the exact opposite of all these Goebbels and Bormanns, those sex maniacs who were only interested in getting them alone in a room. In the Chancellery, at the Berghof, everywhere in the inner circle they were in danger if they were not married. They got pursued, except when they were in the company of the guide. When they went to see him to complain, he advised them to get married as soon as possible and he read the riot act to the oaf who had been bothering them. He told Goebbels off when Leni Riefenstahl complained about his behaviour towards her.

They didn't dare complain about such things to the guide too often – he had other things on his mind. He worried them only when he was having one of his fits of anger or torpor or launched on one of his diatribes against the Jews, but here they were not concerned for their own sake, but for his, for his health, all this energy expended against the Jews, for what? They were neither Jews nor communists, nor were they one of those Prussian generals he hated, so they had nothing physically to fear from him. All he asked of them was to know their place and to spare him their whimsical views on politics.

The Führer enjoyed the company of pretty, gracious women, but he never harassed them. They provided agreeable eye-candy, but he wasn't interested in sleeping with them. He asked after their family and their children if they had any, and it was good if they did. The Führer had a particular fondness for mothers. He loved his own mother like he had never loved anyone since, he wrote in *Mein Kampf*. He carried her photo around with him everywhere. But not that of his father. The young pretty secretaries knew they could be alone with him in his office without risk, they could type up the guide's speeches and have tea without being assaulted.

As for German women more generally, they thought he was single, they found him highly attractive, some of them wrote him love letters every week. He was very much the father of the nation for them, totally devoted to Germany, sacrificing his private life to fulfil his mission. He was married to Germany, it was said, so he was married to each of them, as the guide joked on certain occasions.

Of course, the women in the inner circle knew that the guide hid his own companion, Eva Braun. They knew her, she was a shy young woman, but the more time you spent with her, the more she displayed her mischievous side and her love of partying, champagne and dancing. She was also a maker of home movies, she filmed the guide and his retinue on their stays in the mountains at Obersalzberg, but he hid her. Perhaps he wanted to protect her from the dangers he faced as leader, or the dangers of public life? What is certain is that he did not wish for her to meddle in politics, and she didn't want that either.

The secretaries knew that they must never discuss the contents of the guide's speeches with him. Those women who were sometimes admitted into the inner circle knew that they must never discuss politics with him. The guide considered German women of Aryan stock to be politically irresponsible, like artists.

Margret, Speer's wife, knew this very well. She was waiting her turn in the room in the old Chancellery where she had been invited for the first time. At the initiative of Goebbels.
'My Führer,' said Speer, 'may I introduce my wife, Margret?'

26

A few days later, the guide and the architect met in a more intimate setting; they hadn't seen each other since the reception.

'Speer, why have you never told me you were married?'

He asked this in an intense, serious tone that was inappropriate. The few witnesses there instinctively retreated into their respective conversations. The young architect didn't know what to reply, he blushed and stammered that he didn't know why he had never mentioned his wife.

The question was as implausible as it was absurd, the guide knew he was married, it was impossible that he didn't know, and there was no reason to make a secret of it. And then Goebbels had invited all the wives to this official reception, so Speer being there with his wife was hardly unexpected.

Yet the architect claimed this created an atmosphere of unspoken tension like that between a married couple when one is discovered to have had an affair. And historians have taken this at face value, as they have for most things Speer has said – their writings are based entirely on his own.

At the reception, the guide would not have been able to avoid a somewhat surprised reaction, quickly suppressed by a kiss of the hand and compliments on Margret's beauty, turning to his young architect to say he could see why he had hidden her away from everyone, even him, his Führer.

They were like that, they were men who hid their wives. Something else in common. There is no way to explain this. Some men display them like pimps, others conceal them like sultans.

Eva Braun often locked herself away in her room when important guests flitted around the Berghof, and Margret Speer hadn't seen much of her husband since he had been with the Führer. The architect was very fond of Eva Braun, just as he was very fond of Magda, Goebbels' wife. That didn't mean anything in particular. These were very useful friendships in the inner circle of supreme power in Nazi Germany. The young architect wasn't getting any younger, but he was still handsome and talented, and he didn't chase after women. They soon learned that they had nothing to fear, but also nothing to expect, from him on the physical score.

During the presentations, the guide would have taken the architect aside for a moment to question him.

'Speer, how long have you been married?'
  'Six years, my Führer.'
'Do you have any children?'
  'No, my Führer.'
'Six years and no children? Why not?'

The young architect was lying. Margret was five months pregnant. But he lied to him and felt he had good reason to do so, even if it was absurd. Soon the child would be born, and the guide would know he had been lying. Perhaps he knew already – most doctors were members of the Nazi Party and worked as

SS informers, that is when they weren't actually members of the SS – but the important thing was not to talk to him about it. He felt that no emotion of this kind should trouble their relationship. He felt that so strongly that he instinctively came out with this lie.

Six years married and still no children. The guide himself refused to have any. His devotion to the greatness of Germany closed the door on any possibility of family life, he explained to his entourage with satisfaction. And then, great men usually had disappointing offspring. 'Look at Goethe's son,' he never tired of saying. 'An idiot! Can you imagine if the same thing happened to me?'

Six years married and still no children . . .

Towards the end of the reception, the guide told Margret, in a tone in which she detected, behind the accustomed authority, a certain solemnity, about the importance of a special relationship, which both flattered and alarmed her: 'Your husband will build edifices for me the likes of which have not been seen for thousands of years.'

27

An avenue of wonders lined with wonderful buildings – the guide expressed what he wanted in a few drawings of his own. 'It will be my largest commission,' he told him, 'and my last.'

The architect could see that the austerity of Paul Troost had been totally effaced in the colossal dimensions of these buildings crammed with architraves, cornices, pilasters and various other forms of ornamentation. Troost's neoclassical austerity had dissolved like a sugar cube in the inverted dome of a cup of coffee.

For the architect, this was all sublime, but it was not enough.

Basically, the guide had envisaged an avenue to supplant the Champs-Élysées in the mind of the German and international public. It was inspired by Paris, but also the Ring of Vienna, since like the latter it would contain the major buildings of power and entertainment. Except that it was merely a dizzyingly straight line with a plethora of columns, fountains, statues, domes bearing no relationship to the wider context of the capital.

The guide hated the capital, he reckoned it wasn't one, that it hadn't been conceived as a completely distinct metropolis, like Paris or Vienna. Perhaps this was the fault of imperial federalism, this house of cards built by Bismarck. Fortunately, the Nazi Party had kicked over the Bismarckian house of cards with resonant legislation that deafened the ears of the old Germany like the goose steps of his soldiers. Germany was now divided into *gaus* – districts – each with a *gauleiter* at its head; these were all Party members and functionaries, and all attended the vast lunches or dinners to build the Party-state. This form of administration, modelled on the French departmental system, needed a capital worthy of the name, and at the heart of this it required a nerve centre.

This would include all the ministries, a palace for the Führer, a palace for his presumed successor, Göring, a palace for Goebbels. The Reichstag would be little more than a tiny hunting lodge overshadowed by these new façades and colonnades. There would be the headquarters of the army, palatial barracks for the SS, enormous hotels, enormous shopping centres, masses of stone for masses of flesh, operas, theatres, places of entertainment scattered here and there among the multitude of buildings of power, and they would all be adorned with the eagle and the swastika, displayed to be seen by the world and the people. There were also plans for tanks and cannons configured as public sculptures.

And at one end there would be a triumphal arch – the Führer's pride and joy, his favourite child, which had been in gestation since his youth – two and a half times taller and longer and at least five, maybe six times wider than its model and distant French cousin in Paris, the world's most beautiful city, but not for much longer.

At the other end there would be a dome, but not just any dome. It would be the dome of the German people of Aryan stock, with a cupola large enough to contain St Peter's in Rome several times over and accommodate 150,000 or even 180,000 people at least, who would be able to enjoy concert-hall acoustics while the rest of the German people would be able to listen on the small, affordable radio sets sold and promulgated by Dr Goebbels.

But it was still only an avenue, and in its use of urban perspective nodded at Baron Haussmann and his ideas about town planning. It posed problems of urban redevelopment at vast scale which the guide didn't care a fig about initially, focused as he was on the sheer splendour of this five-kilometre long and 120-metre wide perspective that would surpass the Champs-Élysées in Paris every which way. Paris, always Paris, the most beautiful city in the world according to the Führer, the Americans and the rest of the world.

The architect could see the faults in the plan from an urban planning point of view, but instead of reducing the gigantic scale of the avenue and adapting it to existing Berlin – which would be suicidal, the Führer would be disappointed and would perhaps snub him, to the delight of Bormann and Goebbels – he would do the opposite. He would adapt Berlin to the giant scale of the avenue.

He told the guide straight away that he had to rethink Berlin completely, especially the transport system, build railway stations, extend the main avenue with transversal avenues, gigantic interior courtyards, rethink habitat, traffic and recreation with new parks and lakes.

The guide acquiesced to everything. This amplification fitted perfectly with his amplificatory frame of mind.

They opted for a north–south axis for the avenue: to the north would be Adolf Hitler Square with the dome as its apotheosis, to the south would be the Führer's triumphal arch, and between the two, dozens, hundreds of million cubic metres of ministerial, military, Nazi ideological stone, with swastika standards everywhere setting a rhythm for every breath of the German public, capturing their gaze. If you tattooed swastikas onto every German retina, it would still be less effective than these banners stretching from one end of this avenue to the other.

They set a date for completion of this great work, in the

knowledge that the Führer was obsessed with how little time he had left, as he never ceased reminding everyone at the Chancellery or the Berghof, in front of the spectacular bay window he had designed himself, with its fine steel mesh similar to grid squared pages of an exercise book.

The date was 1950. Perhaps 20 April 1950, the guide's birthday. On 20 April 1950, he would be celebrating his sixty-first birthday.

A childhood, then teenage, then adult dream that had grown into a dream of old age.

28

A dream or at least a childhood game that lasted into adulthood. They quickly made some models. They quickly mounted them on trolleys. Each building had its own. Put together, they formed the whole avenue, which could be shunted around and recombined indefinitely. Lots of adults behave like this. Lots of adults reconstruct battles in their garage in the evenings and on Sundays. Lots of adults paint lead soldiers and set them out on boards covered with moss and branches representing trees, plains and hills. Lots of adults run electric trains across boards covered in papier mâché mountains decked out in moss and branches representing forests. Lots of men remain little boys, playing dolls with their wives whom they treat like naughty little girls who must be punished in the evening. Lots of women remain Barbie dolls until quite late in life, looking for their daddy-Führer to punish them on a whim and protect them from the rest of the world.

That is how it is, and there are even poets and thinkers who celebrate those human beings who grow into adulthood but retain the heart of a child. Children play at soldiers, children become soldiers when they grow up, children crush ants and torture flies, adults crash into each other as they crashed as children in the playground, adults go down into the cellar or up into the attic to reproduce battles, electric trains and their railway network, fighter planes and warships, and the guide was wide-eyed with anger when he talked about the Jews and wide-eyed like an excited kid when he inspected and showed off every part of his avenue of wonders brilliantly illuminated by a spotlight that simulated the passage of the sun.

It must have been around thirty metres long. It consisted of monumental miniatures. Scale was deceptive. Tiny in real life, Goebbels was a giant among them, the guide even more so. The architect and the SS officers surpassed all of them at 1.8 metres minimum, and in this environment of totally white reproductions of buildings destined to become amazing ruins in a thousand years' time, the guide thought that they were titans.

'Speer ... our constructions take precedence over everything ...' he said. 'You must pull out all the stops to complete them in my lifetime. When I have talked there and governed there, I will have sanctified them for my successors.'

He told him this during one of their many getaways, driving across the Reich in a Mercedes convertible. They had just visited a monastery, and the guide had chatted with the prior. They were now picnicking in a clearing next to the road. Everyone was sat in a circle around the guide. He was praising the prior, praising the Church, threatening it, insulting it. He delivered these contradictory sentiments in a single breath of his gravelly, serious voice, held in the back of his throat, almost a whisper, until it burst into a tirade, an invective, as if spat out of a cave.

'That prior ... what a splendid example of the Catholic Church's judicious choice of clergy. Only here, in our movement, can a man from the lower strata rise so high. Sons of peasants have become pope. The Church didn't know social discrimination before the French Revolution. It is paying dividends. We mustn't try to copy it or replace it. Rosenberg and Himmler's dreams of an Aryan Church are ridiculous. Make the Party into a new religion? The gauleiters are not ersatz bishops, and the heads of local groups cannot serve as priests. The people wouldn't go along with it. If this band of "Führers" tried to outdo the Catholic Church in the field of liturgy, they would fail completely. They are not at the required level. It's not easy to create a tradition . . . The Church will have to fall into line. I know this shower of posers all too well. What do they do in Britain? In Spain? You have to exert pressure on them. The buildings of our cult in Berlin and Nuremberg will ridicule the dimensions of their cathedrals. If some little peasant comes to our great dome in Berlin, he won't just have his breath taken away. From that moment on, that man will know where his place is.'

29

'You have gone completely mad . . .'

The architect was saddened by his father's words on the new Berlin, but he wasn't angry. He didn't feel anything any more since he had experienced the world through the guide. The guide made you feel the world when he spoke to you, when he chose you, when he raised you to the rafters in his company. Who could resist that? He had never felt anything before him, he would say. It is only when he was with him that he really felt anything. Neither his family nor his friends offered him such a panoply of exalted emotions.

'My Führer, may I introduce you to my father, Albert Friedrich Speer?'

It was a chance encounter. Father and son were at the theatre, and the guide happened to be there too. The guide noticed the old German standing next to his young architect and asked his subordinates whether it was his father. They told him that it was, so he had them brought over.

The guide sang the praises of his son. He gripped his father's hands and didn't release them, looked him in the eye as he spoke. His father trembled. He was unrecognizable in his son's eyes. He was pale, trembling and didn't say a word, except in order to extricate himself. The father would never see the guide of Germany again, and the son would never refer to this meeting with his father.

30

1938

One evening, at a gathering at the Palace of Arts in Munich, a German playwright saw Hitler and Speer together, surrounded by a host of Party bigwigs. The author was called Gunther Weisenborn. He led a double life. When his works were banned in 1933, he fled to Argentina. He was one of those who left. Then he came back. He had that opportunity. He was now one of those who stayed in the Reich. Officially, he was a minor pen-pusher in a department of the Ministry of Education and Propaganda. Secretly, he was a member of a cell of the German Resistance, risking his life, even at society soirées.

He observed Speer and his Führer, and he observed the Führer and his retinue, the Görings and the Goebbels and gauleiters X or Y. To his eye Speer was different from the others, and it wasn't a subjective impression, it came from the actors themselves. As soon as the Führer said anything about a painting or a sculpture, everyone jumped on board and went into raptures, praising him for the aptness of his comments. And he received these homages from Goebbels or Göring with a fake air of affable bewilderment, his wide eyes moist or quite empty.

But his attitude changed when he turned to the silent and aloof Speer. The Führer leaned in towards Speer, who assumed a rather bored or indifferent pose, perhaps whispering some sharp and brilliant comment. He leaned in towards Speer, his eyes blazing fiercely with expectation and contentment, and Speer seemed to respond with something delivered with all the hauteur of his slim and weary youth, and the guide stifled a laugh. The dramatist Gunther Weisenborn made a note to himself that this Speer seemed to be an object of admiration and love, soaking up the veneration of his Führer as if it were the most natural thing in the world.

A long time afterwards, Albert Speer read Weisenborn's memoirs. He had plenty of time on his hands, he was imprisoned in Spandau. He read this passage in the way one looks in a mirror, surprised to be surprised. He defended himself. He also recalled Hettlage's statement that he was Hitler's unrequited love.

Then literature came to his aid. He employed a quotation from Oscar Wilde: 'Because to influence a person is to give him one's own soul. He does not think his natural thoughts, or burn with his natural passions. His virtues are not real to him. His sins, if there are such things as sins, are borrowed.'

That was reassuring: he had acquired his sins from Hitler. 'Forgive me, Father, for my sins are those of another.'

It is easy to laugh at now, but he was sincere in his moral suffering, and there was nothing Catholic about it. He saw himself as a romantic victim of romanticism, especially of fin-de-siècle decadence, which dabbled in occultism and possession by spirits. He had been possessed by the guide, signed a Faustian pact with him, a disturbing thought for a rational man like him. And Wilde offered him another way out. He remembered Dorian Gray, a dandy who preserved his beauty despite his crimes. But what would have happened if he, Speer, had pasted his moral ugliness over his face? Would he have freed himself of it?

★

Yet another remarkable scene where Speer questions himself and tugs at the heartstrings of lovers and aficionados of literature. Here we are in prison with him, getting carried away by this mash-up of literary references and identifications. Speer, the unrequited love of his Führer, is supposed to be Dorian Gray.

31

1938–1939

The guide followed his young architect, and they were followed in turn by the Goebbels, Görings, Himmlers, Bormanns and other bigwigs of the regime, looking like bridesmaids carrying the train of the bride.

The guide was dazzled. His new Chancellery was simply dazzling, with its different types of marble and perspectives never seen before, not even at Herrenchiemsee, one of Ludwig II of Bavaria's castles designed to reproduce Versailles. And here it was serious, unlike Herrenchiemsee. An elongated Valkyrie reclining like an odalisque on the urban landscape of Berlin. It was long, it took so long to walk from end to end. It was an intermediary between the buildings of the old Germany, which had been spruced up as much as possible by plastering swastikas all over their façades, and those of the new Germany due to be inaugurated in 1950. This was 7 January 1939.

One year earlier, the guide had commissioned his young architect to build this architectural Valkyrie. He needed it to receive diplomats. He needed a new structure to impress foreigners who came to haggle over questions of borders. The architect got it straight away. He knew he wasn't building monuments for a small Reich but for a great one. The architect was not a pacifist. The greater the Reich became, the greater he himself would become. However, the timeframe was very short. In principle, the schedule was impossible. The guide knew that. The architect knew it also. But it brought back a happy memory. Between them, after all these intense years huddled over drawing boards and huge models, the time of memories was merging with the present in their joint history. They remembered the bet that the guide had made with Goebbels concerning his own apartment. They remembered that the guide had bet that the renovation would not be completed on time. The guide had lost.

The commission was made in the early afternoon. A few hours later, the architect returned with a schedule. March 1938: complete the demolition of the existing building; August: complete the outer shell; early January: delivery of the new Chancellery. The architect assured him: 'It's never been done before. It will be a unique performance.'

The architect and the guide knew that the plans had in fact been ready for some time. They had to set them in motion more quickly and on a tighter schedule than originally envisaged. It was a question of speed. Surprise the diplomats at the first glimmerings of 1939. They had to strike fast, like a military Blitzkrieg.

It was now 7 January, two days before the official opening. The guide expected to find bits of scaffolding still standing, that end-of-building-works vibe that he loved, where he could amaze his entourage and the builders with his knowledge of masonry and structural works.

But it was all finished. He could move in straight away.

There have been many retrospective descriptions of this new Chancellery, which no longer exists. They all emphasize its inhuman scale, its famous long sequence of rooms with slippery floors and overbearing dimensions designed to gradually undermine and exhaust visitors even before they reached Hitler's office. Inevitably we overlay it with feelings that were not obvious in 1939. Inevitably we superimpose the extermination of the Jews of Europe on the architecture. The faces of Auschwitz superimposed on the photographs showing the galleries of marble, twice the size of the hall of mirrors at Versailles, and the Arno Breker statues, and the Führer's office with a marquetry dagger half out of its sheath, which seduced Hitler so much that he made eyes at Speer in front of everyone.

And that makes perfect sense, it's actually the moral thing to do, and now, at least for some of us, this superposition is so instinctively compelling that it makes us want to cancel everything, to give up on this book and consign it to the scrapheap.

Damnatio memoriae: the removal of tyrants from our memories practised by the ancients. Never mention their names, erase them from the tablets, prevent them from being reborn. We don't practise *Damnatio memoriae* in modern times, but nevertheless we retain aspects of it in certain situations, for example the disappearance of a dictator's dead body to prevent their tomb becoming a shrine for future admirers. And alongside this, the demolition of some of their monuments. The Soviets razed the new Chancellery to the ground and used the marble and other materials to build monuments to the dead of the Great Patriotic War and a metro station.

On 7 January 1939, the architect, the guide and his retinue walked the famous walk, passing from room to room, each one different in its proportions and materials, creating a sense of surprise like some unfolding theatrical intrigue. The architect in his memoirs described the guide's positive reactions to the slippery floor and the dagger partially withdrawn from its sheath. It is he who makes him speak. He doesn't have him say

You Are the Führer's Unrequited Love

anything else concerning the multiple aspects of the décor that must have been the subject of intensely admiring comments. But he does record an atmosphere of general amazement.

Although on the outside it looked like a military academy of the neoclassical type, especially its very martial courtyard of honour, the interior was neo-baroque. Pomp and circumstance were in evidence everywhere. Most foreign visitors would have found breathtaking luxury and a rare architectural intelligence that would have astounded future centuries. Before the war, in the very short time in which it was in use, their unease, if they felt it, sprang less from the walls themselves than the beings within them, all those SS officers and Nazi diplomats taking them to meet their Führer.

To bring this off, the architect mobilized 4,000 workers, working in shifts, day and night, seven days a week without any break. The equivalent of a very large infantry regiment. Still a somewhat modest workforce, but made up of highly specialized workers. An elite among builders. He took risks and he succeeded. He started some sections of the building before he had finished the necessary calculations to check their feasibility. He knew how to marshal his workers' skills, improvise solutions, and avoid the usual delays that afflict public works. He had organizational talents well above the norm. He also knew this came from his particular situation in relation to the guide.

The guide often held one-to-one meetings. They were known to the inner circle as 'four eyes' meetings. Himmler, Goebbels, Göring, Speer, the chiefs of staff, the ministers all went in one by one to his office in Berlin or at the Berghof, and re-emerged with very precise orders, delivered orally, which they then had to translate on paper in their own departments. His was an oral power, and they often came out livid from these meetings with Hitler, traumatized, convinced, seduced, fanaticized by what they heard. They came out endowed with indisputable power, that of the Führer. They were the Führer's avatars in the theatre of operations.

At least until the outbreak of the war, the 'four eyes' the guide held with the architect had nothing in common with what the other faithful experienced. And it seems they continued that way until the end, through all the ups and downs of their relationship. Their unique complicity raised their conversations to incomparable levels of agreement and disagreement. But when the architect was allocated a task, he possessed the same authority as all the Himmlers, Goebbels and Bormanns. If anything, a greater authority, because of the Führer's special affection for him, which filtered down into all the ministries. This allowed him to cut through rivalries that would have persisted without him. As a result, everything was more organized, which confirmed his reputation as an exceptional organizer.

The guide thought that this new Chancellery was a work of genius on the part of his architect. For the first time, he acknowledged this publicly in his inaugural speech, and he rewarded him like he had never been rewarded before.

32

The young architect was not the only young architect in the new Reich. There were others. In particular, there was a certain Hermann Giesler. He was six years older than Speer, he wasn't handsome in the way Speer was, no Leni Riefenstahl had cut his face out of the newspaper. But he was an architect. Architecture was the guide's passion. All the important members of the Party knew that, the gauleiters, the mayors. That was why they had all initiated building works in their respective towns and regions. Soon there were building sites everywhere. Whenever they visited the Berghof or Berlin to see the Führer, they did so with rolls of drawings under their arms to dangle in front of his eyes. My Führer, would you like to see my plan for a bridge? Would you like to see my plan for an opera house?

The opera, the theatre . . . It was simple. The guide wanted to see an opera house and a theatre in every city in Germany. The guide couldn't resist whenever the theatre or opera was mentioned. Speer couldn't do everything. He had Nuremberg and Berlin. Giesler was given Munich and Linz. Both cities had played a major part in the guide's life. He had lived in Linz between the ages of eight and eighteen. It was there that his vocation as an artist was born. He called it *Heimatstadt*, his home city. As for Munich, it scarcely needed saying.

Munich, the Osteria Bavaria, the early years of the Party, his old comrades . . .

The architect was furious. Why had the guide chosen this Giesler instead of him, Speer? He could have managed not just Nuremberg and Berlin, but at least one or two others as well. That wasn't all. Giesler was also overseeing official construction projects in Weimar, Augsburg and Obersalzberg.

Giesler was the son and grandson of architects, like Speer. Unlike Speer, he was a Nazi from the very start. He had signed up voluntarily at the age of seventeen and had served in the Great War, like the guide. Speer was gripped by fear, despair, incomprehension, hatred, jealousy. His hostility would never relent, even after the Third Reich. Giesler would publish his own memoirs, with no great success, and would continue to work relatively anonymously as an architect in the Federal Republic, but Speer would despise him for ever.

He felt his position, his power, was threatened; his nascent army of workers broken up to this Giesler's advantage. Still a micro-army, a few thousand men under his orders, from all over Germany, but already broken up.

He had been showered with honours so far. His work in the labyrinthine administration of the National Socialist Party identified with the State itself, his work in the National Socialist Party-State made him an important figure, albeit still behind Göring, Goebbels, Himmler, Hess, Bormann, the generals and the ministers. Officially he was the chief architect of the Party, the head of the 'Beauty of Labour' organization, which set out to improve workers' conditions by creating more modern factories, and inspector general of building in Berlin and Nuremberg, with a rank of under-secretary of state.

That wasn't inconsiderable, but at the end of the day, did it amount to much? Was it commensurate with the special

You Are the Führer's Unrequited Love

relationship that he had with the guide? Was it commensurate with the time he spent with him, with their mutual need to see each other and to muse out loud over plans for Berlin and other plans involving the complete rebuilding of around thirty German towns, for which the young architect was not even responsible but on which the guide consulted him all the time because he couldn't do without his advice?

In the labyrinthine organizational structure of the National Socialist Party-State, competences and domains overlapped. Several ministers were often carrying out comparable programmes simultaneously, and their managers clashed with each other more than they cooperated, creating conflicts of authority, muddle, delays, programmes that led nowhere. Himmler built his own army at the expense of the Wehrmacht; Göring had his Luftwaffe and prevented the navy from having a fleet air arm, and he was also in charge of Finance and the police force; Bormann was the official secretary of the Reich Chancellery, where he centralized all the requests of all the organizations and all their chiefs and then thwarted them to serve his own interests.

Speer had skilfully expanded his domain of activity by courting Göring and becoming the master builder of all the Luftwaffe's factories. That had nothing to do with the construction of monuments in Berlin and Nuremberg, but in the National Socialist Party-State that didn't matter, it was possible, and the guide did not have the strength to manage the political/personal conflicts between his minions. He had the strength to provoke them, but not to deal with the consequences. He challenged them to satisfy his demands, they all threw themselves into it, and the administrative confusion that ensued was no concern of his.

The architect developed an implacable strategy to thwart any future Gieslers. He envisaged a single buildings inspectorate whose task was to ensure stylistic homogeneity across all these projects. Otherwise heterogeneity would ensue; the art of the Third Reich could not allow such a flaw, which would be equivalent to miscegenation. The art of the Third Reich measured itself against styles from the past; it should be possible to talk about a National Socialist style, or even an Adolf Hitler style, in the same way one might refer to Greek or Roman style, or Empire or Louis XV style.

And a general inspectorate would, of course, need a general inspector.

And the logical choice of inspector would, of course, be Albert Speer.

The job title would be 'commissioner of the National Socialist Party of German Workers for architecture and urban planning'.

He was a prince and he had no doubt his manoeuvre would work.

In theory, he should have gone to the guide, arranged a 'four eyes' meeting in the afternoon or even the evening, when they were alone together in a corner of the Berghof or the new Chancellery, ensconced in comfortable armchairs he had designed himself.

He didn't do this. He was distracted by all the privileges the guide had granted him over the years.

Almost casually, he wrote a memo detailing how this inspectorate for overseeing the architectural style of the Reich would work. He sent it to the Chancellery, hence to Bormann. All papers went through him, and he made an oral summary of them. The guide virtually never read papers, he listened to Bormann and made his mind up on the basis of what he said.

After listening to Bormann's report, he turned down Speer's proposal.

★

You Are the Führer's Unrequited Love

This was the first false note between them. It was the first time the architect had been spited. It was huge. Of course, he knew that the guide had refused because of that swine Bormann. He knew that going via him had been a mistake. He knew that Bormann had amplified his rivalry with Giesler and distorted his project to make it seem abstruse and all about his ambition, little more than crude intrigue. The guide was annoyed and refused the young architect's proposal.

Perhaps he was mainly annoyed at the unorthodox way his favourite architect had gone about things? Perhaps he was annoyed that he hadn't come to talk to him face to face, as was their usual way? Why had the architect arbitrarily insisted on this absurd administrative distance between them? Why hadn't he come to have a word with him instead of going via Bormann?

No matter, the architect was wounded, stricken by the guide's curt refusal. Thirty years later, his hurt was still apparent on the page. He felt abandoned. He faced this abandonment head on. He was like someone threatening his spouse that he was going to kill himself. He wrote a melodramatic letter announcing his resignation from all his duties so as to concentrate on the completion of the monuments in Berlin and Nuremberg. After that, he would return to being a simple architect working for private clients.

The guide responded that he was totally right, it was an excellent decision, he was free to go. He wanted to leave? Then leave, the door was open! The architect was mortified.

In every way, times had changed. The architect was no longer a priority after 1 September 1939. The remilitarization of the Rhineland in 1936, the annexation of Austria in 1938, the annexation of the German-speaking regions of Czechoslovakia, then its dismemberment the same year, hadn't led to war against the British and French. The invasion of Poland on 1 September 1939 did.

The architect was thirty-four. He was still young, but his relationship with the guide had aged. The guide's snub to his young architect was just the culmination of an inevitable process of ageing. They had known each other for six years now, since that impromptu lunch, not to mention that earlier first interview, the architect with his drawings, the guide with his dismantled revolver. The revolver was now perfectly oiled. The barrel, the cylinder, the trigger, the hammer, had been reassembled. Architecture was no longer a priority despite the guide's claims to the contrary. The architect knew this very well.

Estrangement

(1940–1945)

33

June 1940–April 1945

28 June 1940. At dawn, a Focke-Wulf FW 200 banked slightly in the northern sky of Paris and its portholes framed the view of the French capital, its monuments and its boulevards. It was a four-engined, long-range aircraft first commissioned by Lufthansa for its long-haul flights to New York and Tokyo. It was known colloquially as the 'Condor'. With a few tweaks here and there, it could have made a decent long-range bomber, carrying several tons of ordnance for thousands of kilometres, but the guide did not believe in massive bombardments, which implied a long, drawn-out war. He believed in Blitzkrieg, with tanks and medium and light bombers concentrating their firepower to annihilate the enemy.

Indeed, France had been defeated, and Britain had lost all its military materiel on French soil. Six weeks was all it had taken. Half a season, compared with the four years, three months and a handful of days of the last war. The Focke-Wulf was the Führer's personal plane, and he was looking forward to visiting the most beautiful city in the world accompanied by a few handpicked artists from his regime. Arno Breker and Hermann Giesler accompanied him. Albert Speer accompanied him. At dawn, the Condor landed at Le Bourget.

23 April 1945. A Fieseler Fi 156 flew over West Berlin at low altitude. It was known colloquially as the 'Stork'. The architect was

on board. Since 1942, he had no longer been an architect. He was now the Reich minister of armaments and war production. He observed the smoke, the collapsed roofs, the hideous façades. He observed the fascinating and hideous effects of the massive bombardments on the buildings, the tortured shapes they presented to his expert eye as architect and armaments minister. He observed the formal effects of the bombing raids carried out by long-range, four-engine planes capable of carrying several tons of ordnance for thousands of kilometres and then returning to their base to continue, day and night, their intensive, repetitive, fascinating and hideous work of demolition. The Germans had never developed an efficient long-range bomber. They had caught on too late. The results were stupefying. The cities of the Reich were in ruins. The capital totally so. None of these ruins corresponded to the theory he had formulated.

It was true that the buildings and monuments destroyed had not been constructed following the special directives concerning static physics which formed part of this theory of ruins. It was true that the impact of a bomb manufactured in 1945 was not the same as that of a bomb made in 1934, when he had that quintessentially German romantic dream of building an edifice with a view to its eventual dilapidation. It was true that there was no ivy yet growing elegantly over the demolished columns and collapsed walls. It was true that this theory was absurd like most theories, that it was a concept, an idea, a somewhat intellectual desire, a utopia, and that in a matter such as this, putting it into action would have been a disaster, a violence, a violation of space by the architect who became a minister of armaments. It was also true that the truth, that concept, that idea of the truth, tormented him hugely in the tiny plane on the scale of the Avro Lancasters and the Consolidated B-24 Liberators that had been pulverizing Berlin and the other German cities for the last three years.

The truth. To tell the truth to the Führer and then tomorrow tell the truth to the Allies. How much truth should he tell? He had known for a long time that the war was lost. He knew that Germany had conducted the war in an abnormal manner and had lost. It was unspeakable, the manner in which Germany had conducted the war, and he had known that for quite some time. He knew that the Soviets, the Americans and the British knew it and that they would not forgive. What he knew exactly about this war like no other was a crucial issue for him because of the victors. The Allies would not be content with a victory like that of 1918. That would be impossible, because of the manner in which Germany had conducted this war.

He also knew that history was written by the winners. He thought about it, there is no doubt that he thought about the way in which history would record the role played by Germany and the Germans in this war, and thus the role he, Albert Speer, had played. All the members of the inner circle were thinking about it to some degree. They had grandiloquently and melodramatically evoked the great men of the past at their mind-numbingly repetitive evenings with the guide at the Berghof or the Chancellery often enough to know who wrote history and to think about that, especially since they had realized that the war was lost. They themselves had never tired of stating in their speeches and their diatribes that they would rewrite history from the viewpoint of Aryan Germany. They stated it publicly, and their staff had produced a mountain of paperwork which proved it. They had been trying to burn all this paperwork for several months, to cover their monstrous tracks, which they knew were monstrous, fully aware of what they had been doing, especially in Poland. The war was lost, and the minister wanted to see the guide one last time in spite of the protests of his entourage and their estrangement these last few years. He couldn't help it. The Stork landed on the avenue of Unter den Linden.

*

28 June 1940. The guide and his retinue visited the Opéra Garnier. He knew it by heart. He had studied the plans and descriptions in such minute detail that the actual landmark itself was nothing more than a confirmation of his autodidactic dream. The architect knew that he saw this building as a model to be surpassed in his numerous projects for Berlin and Nuremberg. Giesler knew it too, and he was thinking about Munich, Linz and a few other places. The guide visited the Arc de Triomphe, which he also knew by heart. The previous year, for his fiftieth birthday, the architect had a model made of his very own triumphal arch, like the ones he had been drawing incessantly since his younger days in Munich. It stood four metres high. You could easily walk beneath it. A monster. The guide visited Paris, its monuments, its boulevards, its Champs-Élysées. He was photographed. His architect was never more than a couple of paces apart from him. The city was intact. He hadn't spared Warsaw. But for the guide Paris was the most beautiful city in the world, and he wondered whether he should destroy it. He gave himself time. The dome of the Invalides. The dome of the Panthéon. He liked them so much and he would probably have to destroy them.

23 April 1945. The minister and his orderly arrived at the Chancellery in the midst of the unreal rubble of Berlin. The great dome of the people had not been built and would remain a model for ever. The Führer's grand triumphal arch, his palace, his ministries and the avenue laying them out in academic perspective would never be built. Nor would the Nuremberg complex and the operas and theatres of Linz and Munich. Instead, they built a number of special, unspeakable installations out in the east which they were not allowed to talk about.

A gauleiter among his friends had said to him the previous year: 'Whatever you do, never accept an invitation to visit a camp in Upper Silesia . . . Never under any circumstances . . . There are things going on there that I am not permitted to describe . . . Not that I would be able to describe them . . .' There was no need for him to repeat himself. Speer didn't seek to find out any more.

The granite and marble monuments remained models, signs sketched on the landscape of an era that had been in mental and physical decline for a long time. The slim forty-year-old minister made unkind comments to himself about the guide's physical decline, his big, pockmarked nose, his fingernails, which he chewed in public, his greenish, puffy skin. The guide was almost unbearably ugly. Tentatively he asked himself a futuristic question, a question on everyone's lips, but one which would have made no sense before 1945: how could he have ever been attracted to this man? Their relationship had lasted twelve years. They had shared memories. Their last good, shared memory was perhaps that visit to Paris in June 1940.

The minister did not have the mind of a filmmaker. He probably did not edit together the various scenes of his life in a single film. He was not a genius of montage like his friend Leni Riefenstahl. He wasn't even a genius of architecture, as the guide had claimed. He was a genius of organization and improvisation, an artist in power, everyone recognized it, even the Americans and the British press talked about him. The articles made it as far as Germany and he showed them to the guide with pride. They saw him as the standout managerial brain in a Third Reich in its death throes. An immoral technocrat, for sure, given that he had placed his talent at the service of a bunch of degenerates, but an outstanding technocrat, the kind of man who would succeed in any place at any time, whatever the regime, a useful, polite, efficient and determined man, on top of his brief, never bogged down, a virtuoso handler of numbers and human resources.

All was not lost, he told himself. He could play an important role for the Americans and the British in defeated Germany. His widely acknowledged skills in industry and public works might come in useful in the reconstruction.

The game he was playing now was riskier than ever, and his emotions veered between cold calculation and sudden impulsiveness. His adversaries were many. The Führer, the few members of the inner circle who were still around, the Soviets at the gates, and himself. Himself and his truths, his lies.

He was no genius of montage like his friend Leni Riefenstahl, but that day a web of secret correspondences was forming. The visit to Paris in 1940, the monuments that were standing, the monuments that were lost, the models of a future Berlin, a Berlin in ruins, the dialectical montage of a fallen world and a world projected on paper, dreams and nightmares, the binary, simple, black and white world of good and evil, of survival and shame, of horror and fantasy. He felt a strong need to see the guide again. He arrived at the bomb-scarred Chancellery and went down into the bunker.

28 June 1940. The morning visit to Paris had lasted two hours. That evening, the guide received his architect for a 'four eyes'.

'Prepare a decree for me ordering the full resumption of construction in Berlin . . . Wasn't Paris beautiful? But Berlin must become even more beautiful! I've often asked myself whether Paris should be destroyed. But once we have finished Berlin, Paris will be no more than its shadow. So why bother destroying it?'

34

The architect was not happy.

Power had been slipping away from him since 1 September 1939, when the army entered Poland. He saw the guide less and less. He had been one of the most ardent supporters of the war. Among the inner circle, he had been one of the most eloquent. For the first time, he had stood up to the potentates who considered the Reich insufficiently prepared. Göring and Goebbels were among them, and the architect did not hold back and accused them of being weak and unworthy of the leader and his visions. He claimed to anyone who would listen, particularly his own team of architects, engineers and lawyers, that the exercise of power and its easy pleasures had softened them. 'How he has changed!' his staff and other members of the inner circle who were themselves supporters of the war would say. The young architect knew that a victorious Reich would mean even more sumptuous monuments, where his genius and his influence would come into full bloom.

But now that the war was here and in full swing across Europe, he realized that architecture was only a secondary form of power. He felt useless, he missed the excitement of action. You can't do everything at the same time, destroy and construct, even if the guide wanted it so, and the resources allocated to destroying the enemy were so many resources taken away from the construction of his avenue of wonders, with its triumphal arch and its great dome. And then someone from the Luftwaffe had pointed out that the dome, given its size, would offer an ideal landmark for enemy planes. For all that Göring had boasted that Berlin would never be bombed, the British had bombed it recently, as well as other cities in the Reich. Only a few dozen aircraft, but the experts were saying it was just the start. France had capitulated, but the British Empire had vast reserves of raw materials.

The architect had long discussions with the top specialists in industry and the army. He built up a network of effectively politicized specialists, Nazis, but very different from the self-taught politicians of the inner circle, men who had proven skills in the fields of armaments and organization. And while he had no inside information, he knew that the war wasn't going to end there. He had overheard a conversation one day in that wonderful summer of 1940 when the guide had declared to some generals present that, compared to France, 'The Soviet Union will be child's play.'

The architect had only one question in his mind. What role could he play in this war?

He began by mobilizing his teams of engineers and technicians and offered them to industrialists and the army to rebuild and maintain damaged military infrastructure.

The guide caught wind of this. He was furious. Bormann sent him a letter in the name of the Führer forbidding him from making such moves on his own initiative. How had he dared to do this without informing him, without requesting an interview and sharing his plans? He should concentrate on building new Berlin. The guide was furious that the architect no longer gave these buildings the priority he did before and that he was hobnobbing with military personnel and industrialists at the expense of their projects.

35

Summer 1940–spring 1941

Bormann was the messenger of this verbal fury; he was too large to be Hermes, the winged god who delivered the verdicts of Zeus. He was a bureaucrat, so he wrote a brutal letter forbidding the architect from taking such initiatives and was pleased to see the strutting popinjay disgraced.

One day in August 1940, when the Luftwaffe was conducting its offensive against Britain and incurring heavy losses, the guide suddenly offered the architect the chance to direct military construction along the Atlantic coast.

One day no, another day yes, the guide was like that. Bormann knew it and he shrugged his shoulders. He would nail Speer another day.

The architect was glowing, flattered; the guide still relied on him, and in an area quite distinct from their shared passions.

He also noted how the war increasingly exacerbated the guide's mood swings, which became a constant battle between orders and counter-orders. Some orders were adjourned, others forgotten about entirely, and some executed immediately, with increasingly random results, so it was best never to mention them again. He ordered the architect to continue the building of new Berlin, and thousands of tons of material requiring dozens of trains were earmarked for this ceremonial architecture. Even the architect disapproved of this, though he accepted it. It reinforced his power. He was taking on more and more skilled workers. The guide ordered military programmes, he suspended others and modified most of those that were underway. A fighter plane might be made heavier and become a fighter-bomber, a medium tank might become a big pile of steel, difficult to manoeuvre. There was a shortage of materials, a duplication of skills; Göring was in charge of the four-year plan for the general economy on which the war economy depended, but the latter had a certain autonomy from Göring, so conflicts arose, ambitions clashed and stagnation loomed.

The man who ran the war economy via the Ministry of Armaments and Munitions was called Fritz Todt. He was a German of Aryan stock born in 1891 who had not the slightest nostalgia for the old Germany of his childhood. He joined up in 1914 and fought first in the infantry, then in the air force. He had combat expertise on land and in the air. He was awarded the Iron Cross, and he had worn a swastika armband as a member of the Nazi Party since 1922. He was an old comrade from Munich, a high-ranking officer in the SA and a war specialist. The Führer had a lot of respect for him; he called him Doctor Todt, which indeed was his correct title. He had a doctorate in Civil Engineering, and had written his thesis on types of road surfaces. He was a Nazi, an expert on industrial infrastructure, a 'worldly' antisemite who had gone up a gear and employed some of the team of Walther Rathenau, the minister of raw materials during the Great War. Who happened to be Jewish. Walther Rathenau was a pure German nationalist and a Jew, a genius, a nationalist German of Jewish stock and brilliant, the architect of what was known as total war, that is, the total mobilization of the resources of Germany in 1917 against the enemies of the great Reich of the time. Those who worked with him remembered him with affection, albeit muted, since he was Jewish, but they placed at the service of National Socialism everything they had

You Are the Führer's Unrequited Love

learned from him, Walther Rathenau, who was assassinated in 1922 by antisemitic German nationalists. Speer would later stress Rathenau's importance in his memoirs, and the fact that he was Jewish, implicitly referring to the historical irony that a German Jew should be the creator of the total war that he himself would apply with all his might and which would later be treated as a crime at Nuremberg.

The architect had an excellent relationship with Todt and an ambiguous one with Göring, who loathed Todt, and it was mutual. The architect met Doctor Todt on a number of occasions and offered him the services of his own highly qualified worker army. He now had more than 26,000 workers under his command, all of them highly specialized, not counting the engineers and senior technicians, a wide wealth of expertise covering all aspects of production: military, civilian, underground, railway, river and port. His Berlin Bureau of Construction, the official name of his increasingly tentacular hybrid structure – no comparison to Himmler's, but nonetheless in a sector that was vital for the State – notably built the factories that manufactured one of the most versatile aircrafts of the Luftwaffe, the Junkers-Ju 88, which could be a fighter, bomber or surveillance plane tracking enemy movements at night as well as during the day with a certain degree of success.

The architect was changing, he was like a butterfly, he was a metamorphic creature. In his mind and in his work, the domes had been replaced by the arcs of shells and bullets, and the marble stonemasons and carpenters had gradually given way to the milling machine and lathe operators and the coachbuilders. His earlier predisposition for mathematics had become subordinated to industrial calculations. Little by little he was cherry-picking bits of power here and there, building bunkers and factories, controlling the distribution of certain raw materials. In the National Socialist State, where ministers of Aryan stock encroached on each other's activities instead of working in tandem, where there was a plethora of different directives and models of armaments, instead of a concentration on a few types so as to maximize production, his Berlin Bureau of Construction, his architectural and urban planning practice, became a cross-disciplinary organization flirting with important German captains of industry, scientists and engineers inspired by German Jews who had gone into exile or been assassinated, like Albert Einstein and Walther Rathenau.

And the war continued. Britain refused to capitulate and dealt a heavy blow to Göring's Luftwaffe, investing heavily in the production of long-range bombers and excellent fighter planes, while the guide returned to his first loves. To his passionate hatred of the Slavs, which was beyond compare to anything other than his passionate hatred of the Jews. The guide had turned his eyes towards the Soviet Union.

In August 1939, he had signed a non-aggression pact with the Soviet Union, in which the Germans had exchanged some of their military knowledge for raw materials essential for their fight against France and Britain. France no longer existed, Britain was living on borrowed time, and defeating the USSR would be child's play. That would leave Britain more alone than ever, an old maid, an isolated spinster in the world of geopolitics, at which he had proved himself a genius since the capitulation of France. When anyone mentioned the USA, and the ties between Roosevelt and Churchill, he swatted the argument away with a very longstanding prejudice of his: the Americans were terrible fighters.

21 June 1941. After yet another repetitive, mind-numbing meal, the guide ensconced himself with the architect in one of the

rooms of the Chancellery. He played him *Les Préludes* by Franz Liszt. The opening bars really brought out the acoustics of the space, thought the architect. The guide was beaming joyfully at him. 'You will be hearing this music often, because it is the fanfare that will announce our victories in Russia on the radio. Do you like it? . . . We'll find as much granite and marble as we want there.'

36

February 1942

At Rastenburg, in the east of Germany, in the so-called 'Wolf's Lair', the Führer's main headquarters, the architect told him about his visit to Ukraine, at the southern end of the front, in that very special war the Reich was conducting against the Soviet Union. He had been to Dniepropetrovsk, whose industrial complex lay in ruins. The Soviets were efficiently dynamiting everything behind them. Their territory was so big it was like burning the end of a sheet of paper, leaving the rest intact. He told him about evenings he had spent with the soldiers, nostalgic songs of home, the cold, the ice . . .

The 'child's play' campaign against the USSR was meant to last two or three months, but it was nowhere near its end. Liszt was forgotten. From now on, the concrete music of combat resounded across the planet, no ocean was untouched, the earth's geography was being moulded by battles and blast furnaces. America had been attacked by the empire of Japan, and the guide had declared war on America in alliance with Japan, whose taste for death in combat he loved, the samurai and their suicide ritual, which was strange of him, but no one cared to point it out, the guide's contradictions were not up for discussion. It was strange, because the yellow race was not the white race as envisaged by National Socialism, and even less the Aryan race, but the way they slit open their belly if they failed or as

You Are the Führer's Unrequited Love

a sign of loyalty, their cry of 'Banzai!' with both arms raised in front of them, their veneration of their emperor deeply impressed the guide, and he admired them, just as he admired Islam, believing that Europe and the Aryans had chosen the wrong religion when they went with Christianity, that Jewish sect with a mournful Jew as its figurehead, rather than a prophet sanctifying the sword against the infidels. But that was how it was, the vast majority of Germans of Aryan stock were Christians, he had to deal with it, in peacetime as well as in times when war was raging everywhere on the planet.

German industry suddenly found itself confronted by Soviet, English and American industries, a cruel, angry six-year-old brat facing three overgrown youths high on vengeful hormones. And the 'child's play' of the war in the East was anything but. Never overlook childhood cruelty when it is perpetrated by adults in a dictatorship. Never underestimate the infantilism of dictators.

The architect secretly noticed this more and more when he saw the guide playing with the models of new Berlin, now overdue, or when he heard him talking about the Jews and the Slavs, or when he saw him sullen, bitter, grumbling, incredibly narcissistic, with tantrums worthy of a capricious child, which were disconcerting, as he was an adult and the absolute leader of Germany. Insofar as his anger was directed at the Jews and the Slavs, there was nothing to be worried about, but he was getting more and more furious towards his generals and his inner circle. This wasn't new, there had been others who had been disgraced, like Röhm in the Night of the Long Knives and a few generals who had been coerced to commit suicide, but nothing comparable to Stalin. And when the members of the inner circle secretly compared Hitler with Stalin, they were aware that they were risking their lives much less working for the Führer than they would working for Stalin, with his demented purges, which surprised even the Führer at the time; he treated Stalin like a fool, albeit with a slight hint of admiration in his eyes . . .

And yet his allure remained. When the members of the inner circle and the officers from Headquarters attended his 'four eyes' meetings to tell him a few home truths about the reality at the front and the extent of British bombing of German cities, they emerged newly won over, subjugated once more by his bizarre, almost mythological energy: it was like something from the dark ages, and they knew it was unhealthy, yet it reinvigorated them, to the extent that, at the end, even though the Führer no longer required it, caught up in this increasingly dark operetta, they would give the salute: 'Heil mein Führer!'

The architect had managed to get himself appointed inspector general of infrastructure in Ukraine, the most important of the conquered territories, the breadbasket of Europe. And he had gone to visit the region in his friend Sepp Dietrich's personal plane, a Heinkel He 111, the Luftwaffe's most popular bomber, reconfigured as a transport aircraft. It was an elegant plane, but slow, and it carried five times fewer bombs than a British Avro Lancaster and two times fewer than an American Consolidated B-24 Liberator. At Dniepropetrovsk he admired the town's university and industrial complex and saw the Soviets differently than through the propaganda of Goebbels. This wasn't a trip for pleasure like the one he recently took to Lisbon for an architecture exhibition, not to mention his far too brief stopover in Paris on the way back, where he regretted missing out on the French artists he knew and admired, André Derain and especially Auguste Maillol, a role model for Arno Breker and himself. But the report of his trip to Ukraine, to Dniepropetrovsk, would enliven the evenings of the circle of intimates. Most were incurably sedentary, their knowledge of the rest of the world restricted to office maps or the globe on the Führer's desk in the new Chancellery, so it would be easy to amuse them with his account of his stay among the barbarians of the East.

When he got to Rastenburg, he briefly crossed paths with Fritz Todt, who was totally worn out and depressed. He thought that it was all over for Germany now America had entered the war. Impossible to fight against the three superpowers at the same time. The failure to take Moscow, the winter stalemate, the loss of a quarter of the German forces in the East, the progressive surrender of aerial supremacy in the West were all signs of the inevitability of this defeat. And comparative projections of arms production for each country put paid to any remaining doubt. The architect knew that it would not be a good idea to tell the guide this. Todt suggested that they leave together the next morning on his plane. The architect was looking forward to it.

The evening with the guide dragged on in its repetitive way of old, all the more repetitive since everyone already knew by heart what was going to be said, and the war had left all their faces marked with anguish, the features drawn, the laughter forced. It had even affected the guide himself. It was the first time he had seen him like this. The architect told him of his puny dinners with the soldiers at the front, the homesick songs they had sung; the guide suspected psychological sabotage and he ordered an investigation. A climate of generalized mistrust had set in from the Berghof to Berlin via Rastenburg.

The architect went to bed too late to make the flight with Todt, he told him it was fine to take off without him. Before going to sleep, he felt the satisfaction of having impressed the guide once again with his Ukrainian adventures. As soon as they saw each other, they bonded again, albeit less strongly than before, back when they examined the large plans where he had drawn out the domes and colonnades of the new Reich. Nevertheless, the nostalgia spiced up and enriched their relationship.

He was awoken by the phone ringing. A voice on the line informed him of the death of Fritz Todt. His plane had crashed without any explanation. It was an accident, there was no British fighter involved. There was speculation about who would succeed him. Göring was already on his way to claim the dead man's portfolios.

The guide summoned the architect. He received him formally, which was unusual between them.

'Mr Speer, I am appointing you minister and successor to Doctor Todt. You will take over all of his functions.'

37

February 1943

The Reich minister of armaments and war production Albert Speer was listening to the minister of education and propaganda Joseph Goebbels bellowing to a crowd of men in uniform about whether they wanted total war. It wasn't a real question as there was only one answer. The crowd in uniform stood up and shouted 'Yes!' in response, an archive image that in later decades could be compared without fear of anachronism to the armies of groupies screaming at their idols on stage, whether rock stars, rappers or DJs. You couldn't get more DJ than Goebbels on that winter day at the Palace of Sports in Berlin, just after the defeat at Stalingrad.

The spectre of a violent end to the Third Reich was beginning to take shape, even if hope had not been extinguished entirely. Marshal von Manstein was preparing to rectify the situation in Ukraine. In Kharkov, for the third time, the Russians were preparing to suffer a terrible defeat. And for the last time, the Germans were preparing to carry out a large-scale offensive in the region of the city of Kursk, protruding like a goitre into the German front lines, and by capturing it to crush several Soviet armies once again. Since 1941, the Germans had been crushing new Soviet armies, with the result that there were more than five million prisoners working like slaves in Reich factories twinned with concentration camps. But whenever Soviet armies were wiped out in Smolensk, Kyiv, Vyazma, Bryansk, Kharkov, they were simply reborn. The faces of their troops changed as often as the seasons, many of them now with Central Asian features, a mixture of Chinese and Persian. And no doubt they were reborn in other ways, since in their lands not only was Islam widespread but also old beliefs in reincarnation and other biological mysteries that certain members of the SS studied with passion and fascination in the libraries and particularly the special laboratories at Dachau and Auschwitz. And the inner circle had nightmares about Genghis Khan and his hordes swarming over the beautiful Graeco-Roman temples, raping the Aryan women of Rome and Athens to breed their foreign offspring and plundering the beautiful temples with their peristyles and colonnades, the ruins of which had captivated the guide and his inner circle in those late-night repetitive conversations prior to 1939. For the first time in this war, they had the horrified thought that this could happen in Berlin, Munich, Nuremberg or Linz.

But all was not lost if you could find the means to save what was still capable of being saved. The armaments minister was the instigator of this doctrine, which he borrowed from Walther Rathenau. In the inner circle, Göring had been more or less sidelined since the deadly intensification of bombing of the Reich; Bormann, Himmler and a handful of others had growing influence, and Goebbels had allied with Speer to avoid being reduced in turn to the role of some talking head on the German airwaves.

The only solution, Speer explained to Goebbels, was to place the whole German economy at the service of the war economy as they did in the USSR, America and the United Kingdom. Strangely, National Socialist Germany had not yet done it. Strangely, Nazi Germany was less mobilized than the democracies in the West and the dictatorship in the East. The guide had

You Are the Führer's Unrequited Love

always refused to go there, fearing a reaction from the German people like the one in 1917 and 1918, which led to the abandonment of the army, the betrayal of the front by the rear. The guide was afraid of a stab in the back. He had always had this image in his head of the German army of Aryan stock at the front being stabbed in the back by the politicians, the reds, the Jews and the civilians who stayed behind. The guide was more and more suspicious of his own people through his generals and everything that even vaguely reminded him of the elite. The guide was rediscovering his hatred of the elites, which he had formed in his younger days in Munich, but which he had toned down after 1933, when he started hobnobbing with the Nazified upper bourgeoisie of his new Germany. The guide also refused to allow women to work in the factories, which mobilized a vast number of men who might otherwise have been sent into combat and forced him to have recourse to foreign labour.

When anyone visited the guide, they would find him increasingly livid, tense or elated. He would say yes, and the next day you would find that it was no, or vice versa. He would say yes to you, and the next day you would find out that department X had allowed what the guide had authorized under department Y to fizzle out, so that the blockages and delays multiplied.

Despite this, the new minister of armaments brought about an unprecedented increase in the production of war machines and munitions. The Panzers V and VI, proudly dubbed the 'Panther' and the 'Tiger', heavily clad in steel, with a long gun equipped with an excellent sight, were arriving in the armoured divisions in preparation for the major offensive against the salient of Kursk. Planes were being produced in greater numbers than ever, guns on tracks, submarines, a whole wide range of war machines on land, sea and air, capable of breathing fire, as the phrase had it.

The armies of the various belligerents were working to embody the four elements of ancient philosophy, in the form of tanks, bombers, fighters, aircraft carriers and battleships. Placing the whole economy of the country at the service of the war economy bestowed immense power on its minister. It made him master of the four elements after God, or at least after the head of state.

Albert Speer knew this very well. Some sections of industry and the army already saw him as the most credible successor to the guide, should the latter pass away. He was still young, under forty, still tall and slim, his face had lost that rather juvenile, shy, fierce coldness of a princely Narcissus who devoted his whole attention to a single Führer, that patron of the arts and Pygmalion Adolf Hitler. His was now the coldness of a chief, just as determined as the guide's old comrades, but endowed with a typically old German education and savoir-faire, which reassured the elites, who were naturally repelled by the nouveaux riches from the lower orders of Munich and its bars, all those peasants revelling in their Aryan superiority, yet who clearly did not possess any physical or intellectual qualities.

The minister of armaments was highly esteemed even among the Anglo-Saxon enemy, and he had managed to convert the minister of education and propaganda to the cause of total war. He had him where he wanted him. And when this small, skinny, limping and totally un-Aryan figure asked the crowd if they were in favour of total war, the minister of armaments abandoned all reserve and joined in the general enthusiasm, shouting out 'Yes!' in response, a 'Yes!' intended for himself, Prince Narcissus looking in the mirror and seeing himself as king.

38

Summer 1943

Rastenburg, forest, bunker. They had opened the windows of the room where the staff conferences usually took place. One of these had just come to an end. The Reich minister of armaments and war production was still there, along with a few military personnel who had become members of the inner circle due to the pressure of events. Everyone was silent. It was true that news from the Russian and Italian fronts was not good, and they left these meetings in a state of ever-growing anxiety. Doctor Todt's predictions had all been proved correct. The Kursk offensive had been a fiasco, the Americans and the British had landed in Sicily, and total war would not be enough to prevent the inevitable.

Victory was now out of reach, and even the most optimistic were not betting on a separate peace deal with the Americans and the British in order to concentrate all the remaining forces of the Reich against the Soviets. It was more a pious wish than a thought-through strategy. They were all fully aware of the conference that their adversaries had held in Casablanca the previous year. There would be no separate peace and no pardon for their earlier aggressions. Their enemies demanded the unconditional capitulation of Germany.

The guide went over to a window, turned his back on his guests and looked outside.

Jean-Noël Orengo

'Gentlemen,' he said, 'we have burned our bridges.'
Then he fell back into silence, and everyone did likewise.
Some of the members of the circle knew what he was talking about, and it wasn't Casablanca. They were thinking about the things going on in Poland which they were not allowed to mention. The minister of armaments felt a shudder of horror go through him. He would write about this years later.

39

1942–1943

Spring 1942. A Condor flew over Ukraine. The minister of armaments and SS Reichsführer Himmler were on board. A German fighter ace accompanied them. Down below, they could make out a mass of humanity on the move. The Reichsführer pointed them out and explained: 'Last year, we decided to kill them, but this year we need them for the manufacture of armaments.'

Basically, they were the only two. In spite of the circles of plotters that had formed even within the guide's inner circle, they were the only two. One of them led an army within the army, a state within the state, a police force that he had constantly expanded since becoming head of the SS in 1929. The other led an army of workers, a mixture of salaried German workers of Aryan stock and an enslaved workforce made up of Jews, Soviet, French, Polish, Czech prisoners of war, political prisoners and Resistants, all of them in possession of technical skills that were useful for war production. They were all treated as slaves, the Soviets more than the others and the Jews more than the Soviets, a hierarchy of misfortune that lingered long in the memory like a poison.

The German salaried workers were under the direct command of the minister of armaments, the enormous mass of slaves were under the command of the SS Reichsführer and his camps, and their work under the command of the minister of armaments, a perfect recipe for conflicts of authority and a bureaucratic machine that added more and more deaths to an already highly deadly environment.

In terms of power, the Reichsführer had a long head start on the minister, and the latter was well aware of it. He dealt with him in a polite, pleasant, cold manner – an exhausting exercise as the Reichsführer, an obscene, sinister figure in his melodramatic black uniform, was so unsympathetic. That uniform was no longer the source of private amusement since he had heard certain words in the Reichsführer's mouth, words unbearably brutal to the tender ears of a member of the refined bourgeoisie such as himself.

The Reichsführer issued multiple directives designed to wrest Jewish workers of all ages from the hands of the minister of armaments. The Reichsführer was faithfully following up on the now continual outbursts of the guide against the Jews. He had always said terrible things about them at more or less regular intervals, but as the situation deteriorated on all fronts, he constantly inveighed against them, and the conversations at Rastenburg, at the Chancellery and at the Berghof were virtually about nothing else, apart from recriminations against his generals and frustrated harpings on his failed past as an architect and artist.

The guide's secretaries remembered a day, in March or April 1941, when the Reichsführer emerged from a 'four eyes' meeting with him. Plonking himself down noisily on a chair, he started whining about his fate, something about God and the burden that was demanded of him, without offering anything more specific.

A lot of his subsequent orders were marked 'top secret'. Secrets were everywhere and nowhere in the Reich: you both knew

You Are the Führer's Unrequited Love

and didn't know at the same time. You knew without knowing and knew nothing while knowing everything. The joy, the exhilaration of being German, the fear of not being German enough, the fear of dying at the front or in a bombing raid, the exhilaration of being German of Aryan stock and the rage of killing everything that wasn't, anger, exhaustion, fear of defeat and the consequences of their actions – this was the emotional repertoire of everyone, or almost everyone, in the Reich. Suspicions, rumours, secrets, words both clear and opaque on certain things going on in Russia and Poland were circulating everywhere, among the Germans and the Allies.

Sometimes, the Reichsführer invited VIPs to the camps for a tour specifically designed for them. So the minister of armaments had been able to visit a camp near Linz, linked to the villages of Gusen and Mauthausen. There were a number of granite quarries in the area, and prisoners had extracted stone for his monuments in the days when he was still an architect. Now he manufactured arms. The visits were sanitized of anything horrific lest the delicate eyes and ears of the VIPs be traumatized, even revolted, by the spectacle that actually unfolded there outside of the route specially marked out for them.

6 October 1943, Posen in Poland, approximately 300 kilometres east of Berlin. It was the annual meeting of the gauleiters. The minister of armaments had appeared that morning and addressed them in his capacity as head of total war. He restated and emphasized the absolute necessity of this total war, and that implied total obedience to his orders, which were those of the Führer, and a complete mobilization of all means in the service of this end; there would no longer be any exceptions to the rule. Some gauleiters had ignored this and were running factories producing common consumer goods for German households of Aryan stock under their jurisdiction: that had to

stop. Some gauleiters were behaving like tourists when it came to total war: that had to stop.

The pot-bellied, ruddy-faced gauleiters took it badly; they felt they were being threatened with a spell in a concentration camp. The gauleiters, whose physical resemblance to coarse drunkards had once forced the slim, tall minister and former architect to plunge Nuremberg into darkness and cast searchlight beams into the sky, started shouting as soon as he stopped speaking. Bormann had become the head of the Chancellery of the National Socialist Party, and he was chairing this gathering of gauleiters, linking the various speeches, and when the minister wanted to speak again in order to calm everyone down, Bormann made a sign to him that it wasn't worth it, so the minister had to look on powerless at the anger he himself had provoked in these pot-bellied, ruddy-faced, well-fed and well-housed drunkards. Bormann was happy: he would be able to report this anger back to the Führer.

At the end of the afternoon, the closing speech was given by Reichsführer SS Himmler. He was known to be a bad orator, a purveyor of boredom who sent his audiences to sleep, so the gauleiters got ready to be bored and to enjoy a semi-doze before their night on the tiles.

But this time he had something to say that he had never said before. He said it to everyone present here in Posen, the gauleiters, the regime officials and their ministerial staff, who had turned up in numbers – a large crowd. He said that he had something to tell them about the Jews, and they must never talk about it to anyone else. He said that it was easy to say, 'The Jews should be exterminated,' like they all did over dinner, but it was quite another thing to actually exterminate large masses of people, even Jews, and he knew a thing or two about it, because it was now a fact, between now and the end of the year, the question of the Jewish presence in the territories conquered by the Reich would be dealt with, or almost. He explained that in addition to Jewish men, he had decided to deal with the question of Jewish women and children to make sure that they would not wreak their revenge in the future. He explained that it had been necessary to take the terrible decision to wipe these people off the face of the earth, and it had been the order that he and his SS had found the most difficult to carry out. He reassured them that this had happened without damaging the mental wellbeing of the men and the leaders in charge of the work, even if there was still significant danger of this, since 'there is a very thin line between being cruel, heartless and devoid of respect for human life and being less tough and succumbing to weakness and depression, between Scylla and Charybdis'. He specified that they must always resist the temptation felt by lots of Germans, even Party comrades, to want to save the good Jew that they all knew. He told them that he had received a considerable number of petitions to spare this or that good Jew. He explained that these were often the Jewish workers purportedly helping the war effort in the factories. He gave the example of the Warsaw ghetto, which was kept open too long on the pretext that the workers required for the war industries lived there, and then they had recently revolted. He specified that this reproach did not apply to Comrade Speer, and that he and Speer would in the coming weeks be cleansing the ghettos of these fake workers. He mentioned only Speer in this context of the physical elimination of the Jews, he didn't cite any other member of the inner circle. He finished by saying that they were now informed, that they should keep all this to themselves and, in the name of the German people, take responsibility for the realization, and not just the idea, of the eradication of the Jews from the face of the earth, and that they should take this secret with them to the grave.

40

January–February 1944

A secretary of the minister overheard a conversation through a door. The minister was admired by his secretary, as he was by women generally, they were totally safe with him, he was a handsome, aloof man, indifferent to their personal problems and their crushes. He displayed very little empathy at the loss of their parents in a bombing raid or of their husbands at the front, but he was always very respectful and appreciative of their work and never a danger to them physically or mentally as they negotiated working in this masculine milieu. His exquisite politeness, his brilliant mind, his protective presence made up for all his emotional shortcomings, which they really didn't care about; these were a relief, in fact, devoted as they were to their work in the service at the Nazi Ministry of Armaments and War Production. On this day in early 1944, his secretary was worried, because he was very ill and was struggling to run his ministry and his enormous army of workers. Falling ill meant a loss of power for a minister of the guide, even for him, the favourite.

Previously, when they called each other, on the pretext of discussing the production figures for that month, the minister would end the conversation with the traditional 'Heil mein Führer!', and the guide would respond affectionately with a 'Heil Speer . . .', the only one of the inner circle to receive such a distinction, virtually an invitation to sit at the right hand of power, the place of the son next to the father. No longer.

Previously, the guide would call, and the minister simply had to respond, it was almost a game between them, a friendly ritual in which the most powerful partner – the man of power – always took the initiative to seek out the other, the weaker partner – the man of art. No longer.

Mistakes had been made, bad decisions on the part of the minister, where he had found himself at odds with the guide, decisions that encroached on matters proper to military strategy. The minister had taken the side of generals who were advocating the evacuation of some towns in Ukraine to avoid being encircled and wiped out, as had happened at Stalingrad, whereas the guide was ordering a fight to the death. And the guide had taken exception to this, he had regarded his minister differently after he had taken the side of the hated generals against him, his Führer, his patron, his master. He had felt betrayed, hurt by the one who remained in his heart the architect of his dreams of domes and triumphal arches.

The minister had continued his mission, noting the guide's withdrawal of favour, his unprecedented coldness towards him. He hadn't shown his suffering, his nostalgia for the time when the Führer displayed his affection by calling him on the phone or receiving him impatiently, even after he became minister of armaments, a position less romantic than that of architect.

The guide became distant, the minister suffered and didn't show it, but he kept his distance too. They would see who came crawling back first. He was haunted by prewar memories, they were good, like peace. One day at the Berghof, at a feast, he had caught the guide staring at him for no obvious reason and he had held his gaze. He had treated it as a child's game, an ambiguous game, fraught with tension, where the first to back down was the loser, or at least submitted to the other. And the guide had averted his gaze first, allowing the architect to win.

But now there were different memories.

The minister had seen something for the first time that he would never forget. He had seen an underground workcamp manufacturing rockets where highly qualified prisoners had been reduced to skeletal slaves spending eighteen hours a day on assembly lines in filthy caves, eating foul food and sleeping in foul cubby holes inside the underground factory. You had to step over rotting corpses lying on the ground to reach the workshops. When he had wanted to go into the bowels of the cave, he was told it was like Dante's Hell, but he had wanted to see for himself, and his delicate eyes had been revolted by what they saw. No film, no music, no book could express such things. The words that described them became obscene, suddenly tainted with an obscene pretension, an obscene artifice, as soon as they were uttered, committing them to memory. The torments were reinvoked in the words summoned up to remember them or *make use* of them, the dividing lines were so thin. It was a vicious circle: this must never be forgotten, but memory involved using words, and words had their own laws, and they were ambiguous, even when describing crimes. That was their moral force, to be ambiguous, to operate between two worlds – truth, fiction – and which is the most powerful to read, which is the most appealing version of the facts? The same words were used by lawyers, historians, politicians, novelists, poets, artists, journalists, victims, torturers, and they were also used by the memoirist Albert Speer, artist and minister of the Third Reich.

Since that unfiltered visit, Speer had been visited by the vision of these highly qualified slaves in the workcamp manufacturing rockets for military use. He was horrified to see himself reflected in the mirror of this camp wearing the uniform of

You Are the Führer's Unrequited Love

the guide's favourite minister. He was horrified to be associated with this camp that manufactured his weapons. It was one thing to theorize about romantic stone ruins, it was quite another to see the physical ruin of human beings. This was exactly what Reichsführer-SS Himmler had said about the extermination of Jews and his concern for the mental health of the executioners. Albert Speer was mentally ill, and his illness manifested itself physically in a swollen knee and a chest infected with pus.

The minister was now in a room in a hospital run by an SS doctor in the suburbs of Berlin. His health had deteriorated since he had arrived in this medical paradise, hoping to be cured of this camp, where a special illness had infiltrated him through his eyes, the physical symptoms of which were just the tip of the iceberg. His secretary was staying by his side. She was resting in a room, a conversation was taking place behind the door, she listened, she was horrified. She heard a voice she recognized. She heard Reichsführer-SS Himmler say to the doctor: 'In that case, he is dead.' She didn't catch the response of the SS doctor but she clearly heard the reply of the Reichsführer: 'Enough! The less said, the better.'

The guide told his entourage that his beloved Speer was probably dying. He also told Margret, the wife of his beloved minister of armaments. He talked about it in a tone of satisfied, strangely voracious sadness. Death was part of life. Like when he had to put down a dog occasionally to bring an end to its suffering. Had he thought of having his ex-architect put down, given the ruinous state of that once slim, tall, ideal Aryan body?

One night, his illness took a turn for the worse, his fever rose, he began spitting blood, his skin turned blue, he began to haemorrhage. He fell into a coma. Suddenly he floated to the ceiling.

He could look down on his inert body surrounded by SS nurses and doctors. He could see his wife. Everything was radiant and magnificent: the hospital room had been transformed into a huge white room with a ceiling encrusted with magnificent and radiant decorations, the walls were the white of ecstasy, not the white of medical hygiene, and he breathed the air of Paradise. He floated, and everything floated around him, and he was not alone with the SS staff and his wife. Some vague figures dressed in white and grey floated with him and music filled the room. A detached voice said to him: 'Not yet.' He protested, he wanted to stay with this celestial ballet, and the voice repeated: 'Not yet,' and it invited him to return to that stretched-out, suffering body, and he had a sense of loss as he re-entered this envelope of painful flesh.

He had just had a *positive* near-death experience, a phenomenon observed by anaesthetists and surgeons when a patient slips away from them but then revives, no one knows how, and sometimes tells of having this sort of experience. It is always beautiful, this foretaste of Paradise.

Other, less frequent accounts tell the opposite. Floating, a tunnel, a trapdoor, smells of pestilence, frightening presences, Hell. These accounts are less heard-of because people don't share them, they want to forget, they keep them to themselves. These are *negative* near-death experiences and they are just as common as the positive ones, except that they are more overwhelming. Their protagonists wonder in terror why this has happened to them, when others get to know the ineffable happiness of visiting Eden. These experiences indicate nothing about the past lives of those who go through them, the architect would be delighted to learn later. Torturers might find themselves in Paradise, innocent victims in Hell. There is no rule about it, it is as if the divine justice promulgated in holy scripture were just a huge joke, like the ones of the Führer's inner circle when they cruelly mocked some subordinate to spice up their exhausting and repetitive evenings with the guide. It is as if injustice were the true meaning of this earth, as if injustice prospered even more after death, and misfortunes of virtue or truth or goodness came on once the heart was extinguished, the brain burnt out and death pronounced. It is as if our actions here on earth, whether good or bad, mattered little. In the hereafter they don't count at all.

The minister would claim that he never feared death again after this experience. He knew that happiness awaited at the end of the journey, at least his. In the meantime, it was important to live as well as possible, which he had always done, by adapting to circumstances, whatever they were.

He recovered gradually, a new doctor took over; he was from the SS too, but he was the guide's man rather than the Reichsführer's, and his health improved. He convalesced in a very beautiful castle near Salzburg, where the guide himself stayed. Though it was wartime, this was la Dolce Vita, and he never tired of describing how luxurious these resorts were.

When the guide saw him again, he noticed a change. The minister's reaction on seeing the guide was imperceptible, except to him, the guide. It was as if he were looking at someone else. His Albert Speer had never looked at him in this way. The guide had come on foot, walking across the park and the woods that linked the residences, and been received strangely – no animosity, even some deference, everything seemed the same, and yet nothing was like it was before.

    He came to see him several times for no particular reason. He brought him flowers. He sent him messages that went beyond normal friendship. It was the same thing: everything seemed the same, nothing was like it was before, his Speer had never looked at him like that.

It was a deep crisis between them. The minister was being distant, or else the minister was testing the guide. For those in the circle their little drama was a dismaying spectacle, a whimsical operetta in the midst of tragedy.

It was a drama in which the minister was no longer afraid to stoke disagreement. He would send quite provocative messages without compunction. The guide wanted to construct six large underground factories; the minister opposed this, he felt that they didn't have enough time given the exigencies of the conflict and that repairing bomb-damaged factories would be quicker than building new ones. The guide rejected this, and the minister announced his resignation to the guide via a third party.

The minister felt that he was capable of anything. He had felt abandoned, marginalized these last few months, and now, since his recovery, he had been filled with a sort of intoxication, he felt capable of anything. Freedom, anguish, expectancy and excitement were the dominant emotions that fuelled the minister's provocations of his guide.

Göring called and told him that no one resigns from the Führer's government; others told him that the guide and especially Germany needed him.

The guide sent some magic words via an intermediary: 'Tell Speer that I love him just as much.'

The minister replied to the intermediary that the guide 'can kiss my ass'. The intermediary blanched at this: 'Even you, Speer, can't say something like that to the Führer!'

★

In the end, the minister went to the Berghof and requested a 'four eyes' meeting. The guide suggested one of those repetitive walks that the minister knew by heart. For the first time, the minister refused to go for a walk with him and his dog. He wanted a one-to-one meeting without witnesses or outdoor distraction, a 'four eyes'. He was self-confident, anguished, provocative.

The guide accepted and received him formally, in full uniform, ceremonial gloves and trappings usually reserved for foreign guests. No one knows what they said to each other in their 'four eyes'. When they came out of the room, their reconciliation was obvious, their relief public. It was a return to grace for the minister. The telephone calls were reinstated, distinguished foreigners wanted to make his acquaintance, Bormann invited him to his house for the first time.

Things seemed to be back in place, as before, better than before, as if they had worked through the crisis together, but nothing was the same any more.

From then on, whenever the minister encountered the Führer, he saw nothing but a 'frightful head', a monster endowed with a 'ghastly big nose', bulging eyes and 'rough, pale skin'.

Separation

(1945–1947)

41

Late March 1945

The guide expected his reply before morning. Yes or no, did he believe that victory was still possible? The meeting was at an end. The minister was dismissed from the Führer's bunker without having made any such declaration. It was two o'clock in the morning in Berlin. Above, the Chancellery he had built approached its ruinous destiny under the waves of Soviet, American and British assaults.

The minister had arrived in the late evening. The military staff behaved awkwardly with him, they forgot the basic courtesies his rank demanded. They now felt compromised if they greeted him. He had already experienced this. This was not his first potential disgrace.

The guide received him and went on the front foot immediately. The guide knew that the minister had refused to obey the order to destroy all German infrastructure before the advancing Soviets, Americans and British. He had refused to apply his scorched-earth policy by means of 'incendiary explosives or demolition'. The guide knew from Bormann that his minister had betrayed him. He spoke in that low, calm voice that often accompanied some of his worst moments, when he might send you to face a firing squad or, worse, to a concentration camp.

*

It was almost the same voice that he had used to talk about the German people and the country as a whole in the early hours of 19 March. He had received the minister after a staff meeting to offer him a photo of himself with a dedication in a spidery hand, typical of his illness, which made some of his limbs tremble since he was no longer in control of them. His minister was celebrating his fortieth birthday, and the guide's words came slowly, barely intelligble, but warmer than ever. The minister had been embarrassed for a moment. He had been about to deliver yet another of his desperate memos in the attempt to make the guide give up his scorched-earth policy. The guide had realized this without even reading it and had bristled. Before he left, he had said: 'If the war is lost, the German people are lost too. There is no point in worrying about the conditions needed for the basic survival of the people. On the contrary, it is better to destroy everything. Because the people have revealed themselves to be the weakest, and the future belongs exclusively to the people of the East, who have shown themselves to be the strongest. Those who remain after this war are the mediocre ones, for the good ones will have fallen.'

'Hitler is a criminal,' the minister had declared straight after this interview to a half-asleep colleague in an apartment that they shared at the Ministry of Armaments. He had turned up at five o'clock in the morning, sitting noisily in a chair and staring at the wall, his tall frame bowed, his expression frozen momentarily in a look of insomnia and unhappy thoughts. In his uniform he looked just like one of those German soldiers who were retreating on all fronts. 'Hitler is a criminal.' The day before, they had criss-crossed the west of Germany, at least the parts of it that remained under their control, sitting on a hill, contemplating the undulating landscape full of the smells of spring, a scene typical of German romantic painting and poetry. 'How can he want to turn all that into a desert?' the minister had asked himself out loud before his colleague. 'I won't let him do it.'

And he had not ceased to roll out measures to prevent the destruction of infrastructure, factories in particular.

Bormann had been aware of this. Bormann had been assiduously compiling the rap sheet against Speer, especially since 20 July the previous year. The minister was spending the day with Goebbels when they had learned of the attempted assassination of the Führer by a group of army officers. They were meant to attend the funeral of Leni Riefenstahl's father, but they had cancelled. The attempt had failed, thousands of opponents new and old, real or assumed, had been executed, more precisely hanged from butcher's hooks, after being disfigured in various ways by their interrogators. The SS men in charge of the task had been in their element: beating up the top brass made a nice change from all those Jews they had been killing for so many years. They had even made a film and taken photos of their final agonies, dreadful images of people that the minister had known and whom he had refused to see in this state. His name had erroneously appeared on a list of provisional government ministers found in the files of one of the conspirators.

For that alone he should have been hanged from a butcher's hook. He was still alive. Bormann and others noticed the guide's coldness towards him, and they saw in that a hint of his downfall to come, but he was still alive, still provocative, still writing his foolish memos to the Führer, which were more like letters, mixing the professional with bizarre, completely inappropriate personal effusions.

He had openly disobeyed the Führer in these last few months, and he had even secretly imagined killing him after their interview on 19 March. For two weeks he had thought about gassing the guide via the ventilation ducts of the bunker that opened out onto the garden of the Chancellery. He had abandoned the plan in the end because of recent modifications in the ventilation system that had made it unfeasible.

Another revelation of his memoirs. None of his closest contacts had known anything about it, even after the fall of the Reich. Gassing Hitler. It seemed like typical inner-circle humour, one of those 'ironies of history' they were so fond of.

Now it is our turn to fabulate on this fable. We are inside the head of Speer around 1967, when he wrote these words about his fantastical assassination plan. He laughed. He was amusing himself. He would gas his guide, his master, his intellectual lover. 'Hey, my Führer, here's a gas pellet for your lungs! You have disappointed me, all those bad choices that have led to our defeat, all those thousand-year dreams that you set up only to smash them, you old fool! You've left me no choice. I have to rehabilitate myself, socially, morally. Only the superman survives. So I will gas you, you who gassed the Jews. At least I will say that I thought about it. Even you would have laughed at my strategy, back in those interminable, unforgettable nights at Berchtesgaden! Do you think, my Führer, that my readers will understand the second-degree magnitude of your gassing? Or how much I take the piss out of them, like we took the piss out of Chamberlain in Munich?'

It was the last week of March when he saw the guide again, and the latter confronted him immediately for disobeying his orders for the total destruction of Germany ahead of the advance of the Americans, the British and the Soviets.

They were alone together in the office. The minister saluted him with a 'Heil mein Führer', the guide did not offer him his hand.

His voice was calm and low, dangerous, as the minister well knew, but he wasn't worried. He was exhausted, sure of himself, convinced that he was taking a big risk yet risking nothing. The cocktail of emotions he was feeling had changed in nature; it was richer, more nefarious, but still mixed in there were old feelings from the past, still audible, which told him he risked nothing, that he was the guide's favourite, the favourite of a criminal, the favourite of a Pygmalion, the favourite of an ogre with bad skin and an enormous nose.

The guide calmly laid out his indictment. 'I received a report from Bormann about the meeting you had with the gauleiters of the Ruhr. You encouraged them to ignore my orders, declaring that the war was lost. Do you know what that means?'

He hesitated, the minister sensed he was being visited by memories, and that perhaps suddenly unexpected, indelible memories were flooding back. 'If you weren't my architect, I would have to carry out the consequences that inevitably follow in such a case.'

'Carry them out, then,' the minister replied.

The guide was flabbergasted. His minister must be suicidal. Could he be using the prospect of his own death to blackmail him?

'You are unwell and overworked . . . I have therefore decided that you will take some leave, effective immediately. Someone else will run your ministry on your behalf.'

'No, I feel in perfectly good health and I will not take leave. If you don't want anything more from me, you only have to remove me.'

'I don't want to remove you. But I insist that you take leave immediately.'

'I cannot fulfil my responsibility as a minister while another takes my place . . . I cannot, my Führer . . .'

'You have no choice . . . It is not possible to remove you! . . .

For reasons to do with . . . domestic and foreign policy . . . I can't give up on you.'

'It is not possible for me to take leave. While I am in post, I am the one who will run the ministry. I am not ill!'

They fell silent, the guide sat down, the minister sat down too, without being invited.

'If you can convince yourself that the war is not lost,' said the guide, 'you can continue to carry out your duties . . .'

'You know that I can't . . . The war is lost.'

'If you *believe* that the war can still be won . . . If you were able at least to *believe* it, that would be enough.'

'With the best will in the world, I can't. And besides, I wouldn't want to be one of those bastards in your entourage who tell you they believe in victory when they don't.'

'We have to believe that things will work out. Do you still hope that the war might end in success? Or is your faith shaken? . . . If you could at least *hope* that we haven't lost! You have to hope . . . That would be enough for me.'

The minister gave no reply.

'You have twenty-four hours!' the guide snapped. 'Think long and hard about what your answer will be! Tomorrow, you will tell me that you *hope* that we can still win the war!'

42

He returned exhausted to the ministry, composed a twenty-one-page response in handwriting that was as febrile and indecipherable as the guide's. He evoked their shared memories, the good memories. He invoked the need to save Germany's industrial future and the life of the German people. He invoked art. He had run his ministry as an artist like the Führer had run the Reich as an artist. That argument pleased him, and he knew it would please the guide enormously. Two artists in government, it was much better than two politicians wielding a pen or paintbrush. He finally invoked God: 'God protect Germany!' he concluded.

He phoned the Chancellery to ask a secretary to type the letter out on a special typewriter with large characters adapted for the guide's failing eyesight.

Request refused. The minister had to appear in person.

He set out for the Chancellery at midnight.

Thoughts, hallucinated internal wanderings in a bomb-cratered Wilhelmstrasse.

The bunker.

'Well?' asked the guide.

'My Führer, I stand behind you unconditionally.'

The guide almost had tears in his eyes. He held out his hands to him in silence.

43

23 April 1945

He arrived at the bomb-scarred Chancellery for the last time. It was the end, no doubt his masterpiece, not in stone but in words, when he described the fall of the Reich in his memoirs, a version that became canonical and has been taken at face value by artists and historians with good reason: he knew all about ruins, he was at home with them, he had theorized them in 1934 and experienced them in 1945.

The long suite of rooms was full of debris. Officers were getting drunk, much like elsewhere in what was left of Berlin, from the ministries to the large hotels. They were feasting on the vast stores of food and drink amassed during the years of pillaging all over Europe, especially in France and Italy, where the cuisine was excellent. These parties bore no comparison to those during the years of the 'System', the ones in the cabarets and nightclubs between 1929 and 1932, when the crisis added an extra intensity, according to those who were there. But no matter, he hadn't really known them, he never went to that kind of place with Margret. He wasn't a party-goer; if he had been going to bed late these past twelve years it was purely to adapt to his master's timetable, living at night like a vampire, endowed with supernatural virtues, or rather vices, which turned whole crowds into sleepwalkers. The image pleased him, like the one of Faust making a pact with the Devil. He knew he would be judged by history and the historians of the victory, and he experienced the shame of defeat, not to mention a feeling that he couldn't describe, something like those ersatz products from before the war, a composite feeling in the way that some materials are composite, a mixture of shame, guilt, a thirst for respectability, a will to survive before posterity, to create a persona that was not just that of a monster in the service of a monster and a monstrous regime; so what was he to do? How to go about it when he wished, one last time, at any cost, to see this monster, his guide, his patron, his artist-chancellor? Construct a 'romantic' image of himself? Wasn't he the very model of the artist ensnared in the horror of power because of an outstretched hand – alas!, the hand of the Devil?

His spirit was no different from the Berlin whose charred landscape he had crossed by plane and then by car. His spirit was a field of ruins.

Most of the dignitaries had left, all his rivals had fled straight after the guide's birthday three days earlier. He had visited Göring many times in the past two years in one or other of his luxury residences, where he had seen him cross-dressed, with painted nails, make-up on his face, body wrapped in a kimono, his speech slurred by morphine, and Göring had fled. Despite his grotesque black uniform, Himmler had fled. Apart from a few last-stand generals and a few underlings required to transmit the increasingly random messages to the outside world, only Bormann and Goebbels remained.

And he, Albert Speer, was the only one to return for no good reason, with no work to do – no armaments were being produced, the German military-industrial complex of which he had been the Führer in the name of the supreme Führer had been in disarray for some weeks now. In the streets, children destroyed Russian tanks using Panzerfausts, effective grenade launchers, the ultimate work of that Faustian German genius, not one of those wonder weapons vaunted by the propaganda – most of which were technical chimeras that baffled the engineers – but an easy-to-handle weapon that could be produced on a large scale. He had seen these so-called wonder weapons in the camp the previous year, when he stepped over the corpses of highly qualified slaves who were making rockets capable of carrying a ridiculous payload of explosives and costing a fortune in comparison to the thousands of American and British bombers dropping 4,000 ton of bombs a day on the Reich. There had been fantasies about so-called 'death rays' and other fatuous laser-based weapons. Scientists working on splitting the atom, which the minister had been following closely, had seen their grants cut on the pretext that their work was based on that of the German Jew Albert Einstein. He had all these technical files, all this junk in his head as he walked through his ex-new Chancellery now partly demolished by American and British four-engine bombers, not to mention the admittedly less effective Soviet artillery.

The Red Army encircled Berlin, its troops advanced, attacked by teenagers from the Hitler Youth, to the delight of filmmakers and novelists of the future, predicted Goebbels, who was gauleiter of the city and thus one of the commanders. Had he not motivated his colleagues, with his usual deadly irony, by declaring that now was not the moment to be cowardly, that these final hours would be the subject matter of some excellent films in fifty or a hundred years' time, when the effects of the defeat would have been wiped away by the folly of their political, artistic and martial adventure? The Assyrians and Babylonians had decorated their walls with the skins of their enemies, who had been burned alive. And yet all anyone remembers is the splendour of Babylon and its hanging gardens, not to mention

Sardanapalus and his whims. That's how human memory worked, it was perfectly amoral, it couldn't give a damn about dead and tortured flesh, it even wrote epic poems about it, it forgot names except the names of great men, whether good or bad, because they knew how to seize power and embody it in radical ways, slaughter and monuments, and it loved stone, it would rather be stone than flesh. That was how Goebbels saw things.

'Act as if you are being filmed!' was his credo for both children and adults, the young kids and the old men with Panzerfausts jammed to their shoulders.

One of the drunken officers received the minister and dashed off to announce his arrival. He returned quickly with the banal message that he had heard thousands of times and that was quite familiar to him, the architect and minister of the guide for twelve years, not so much an order, more a request for a meeting: 'The Führer would like to talk to you . . .'

44

'Should I stay here or take a plane to Berchtesgaden? What do you think? The day after tomorrow, it'll be too late.'

The air in the guide's underground office was thick with dust and neglect. The discipline of the remaining soldiers had broken down in a few days. No one stood up now when the guide arrived, they carried on talking, they got drunk in his presence, and the hygiene of the place was getting more and more dubious. Apart from the pointless staff conferences, he spent most of his time with the women of his entourage or alone at his desk.

The minister descended the steps, he was greeted politely by Bormann. He had known that he wasn't in any danger. He had always known it. The only fear he had ever had in twelve years was of losing the guide's affection and all the privileges that went with it. But mainly to lose his affection. He had come back for that attachment, their bonds that went beyond the shame and horror.

Bormann asked him to convince the Führer to leave. He almost begged him. The minister savoured Bormann's fear, his fear of dying. He left him hanging; and, faithful to the spirit of the inner circle, with their love of cruel japes, he enjoyed the secretary of the Chancellery's fear, enjoyed his fear of dying.

★

And now the guide's question. Should he stay or should he leave? He didn't need to think about it. The guide was expecting only one answer, and the minister gave it to him straight.

'You should stay in Berlin. It is better, if it has to be, that you should end your life here as Führer in your capital than in your weekend house.'

45

'Eva Braun would like to talk to you . . .' The servant, an SS soldier appointed to housekeeping duties at the Chancellery, delivered the request, which he hastened to respond to. The minister had a soft spot for her, with no ulterior motives. He would never have looked twice at her if she had not been the guide's companion, any more than he would have noticed Bormann or Goebbels if they hadn't been members of the inner circle. But the fact that she was this secret, naughty companion, a sort of Heidi who had wandered into a Faustian tale, made her noticeable, maybe the most noticeable of them all. He admired her loyalty, her modesty, her shyness, her irrepressible good nature amidst the seedy machinations of the inner circle. They were so pleased to see each other. He inspected the room where she was living, approved of her taste, and why wouldn't he? He had designed the furniture himself years earlier – seats, dresser, table – and she had had them brought down from the small apartment designed for her in the Chancellery upstairs.

She had returned to Berlin to be by the Führer's side. She couldn't stay any longer in their alpine home in Berchtesgaden. She shared his destiny and she harboured no bitterness or fear, quite the contrary. She told him how much the Führer had loved the fact that his minister and architect had returned to them. She had reassured him incessantly: 'Speer will come back.' And here he was. And he had liked what Speer had said about 'taking his bow' here in the capital. It was worthy of their repetitive and mind-numbing autodidactic conversations about Wagner and other sundry Siegfrieds.

She offered him biscuits and champagne, a bottle of Moët et Chandon. She was the first and only person who had thought of his stomach since his arrival, a delightful detail, a true, romantic and vaudevillian little fact amidst all this concrete oozing defeat, not that that bothered her. She had lived a good life, had never done anyone harm, had only loved the Führer, who had never cheated on her – overprotected her, maybe, but never cheated – unlike most of the men of the inner circle, whom she detested, Bormann and even Goebbels. On the other hand, she loved this brilliant, slim architect turned minister because he had never been that sort of man, had never cheated on Margret, his self-effacing, distinguished wife, who had borne him six lovely children.

He listened to her with all the affection he was capable of, remembering how she had been in tears in the spring of 1943. She had just confided in him something normally only shared with girlfriends, not with men, not even homosexuals, men who were inoffensive to women. It was strange to share something like that with the minister of armaments and war production of the Third Reich, but that's how stories go, their very implausibilities have a crazy charm of their own, even in memoirs and autobiographies.

So she had been in tears: the Führer had told her he was no longer able to satisfy her. As a man, he could no longer satisfy a woman's desires, he was so sorry, his duty as war leader took so much out of him with its continual burden of torments and fatigue, and he begged her to find someone else. The worst of it had been this request to go and satisfy her female desires with another. She had cried a lot and turned down this indecent proposal from her Führer. She had also learned some terrible things concerning certain places in Upper Silesia and elsewhere and of the fate of certain people, whom she never identified as Jews, and she felt horribly anguished about it. And she had thought no more about it as she went skiing or, when the Führer was away, danced innocently with young officers who were unaware of her identity. Years had passed, and she was now at peace, full of joy to be here, in the bunker of the man of her life.

They parted around three in the morning. The minister would take his final leave of this underground world where all that came from the outside were rumours and treachery. Göring and Himmler were traitors for claiming power, believing the guide to be already dead in Berlin. Well, he was still alive, counting the hours to his revenge and his coming suicide.

The minister would not commit suicide with him and the small number of the inner circle who were determined to share his fate. He could have done, he liked imagining things knowing that they would never happen, like he had always known that he ran no risk as far as the guide was concerned. He would later refer to a plan to escape on board a state-of-the-art submarine to a secret base in Greenland, where he would have written his memoirs and skied in a crystalline world against the backdrop of the Northern Lights while waiting for things to blow over. And indeed, in the late 1960s, this occultist and horrifying image of Nazis still living in secret ice-bound bases was a staple of popular entertainment.

46

'Ah, you're leaving. Very well. Goodbye.'

They shook hands with no great display of emotion. At that moment, as they faced each other, the minister no longer felt anything, except perhaps the desire to get out once and for all. He was pleased he had come, but pleased to leave again.

They hadn't gone like children or ghosts to pore over the models of the great Berlin, which the guide had decided to rename Germania around June 1942, just as the Allied bombers were beginning to rain down their punishment from the heavens. They had been moved out a long time earlier and stored safely far away from the fighting. The only models still kept at the Chancellery were those for buildings planned for Linz, and these were the work of his rival Hermann Giesler. During the last few months, the guide had often taken guests to examine them in the cellars where they were stored and had sung the praises of Giesler. The minister's despisal of this man had not diminished, but right now the only thing on his mind was to get out of Berlin before it was too late. It was unthinkable that he should fall into the hands of the Russians. His aim, in common with most of the inner circle who had fled before the advancing Soviets, was to give himself the best chance by surrendering himself to the Americans or the British.

47

It is a historical and geographical truism: we experience events simultaneously, we experience them according to where we are on the globe, our point of view is relative to our spatio-temporal location. This is almost a simplification of the Theory of Relativity of the German, then stateless, then Swiss-Austrian, then Swiss-American Albert Einstein, whose life experience echoed his work when, in 1933, his ship crested the curve of the horizon, carrying its passengers into forced exile.

It is a simplification which contributed to some of the great novels of the first half of the twentieth century, in which different characters simultaneously experienced the same mundane events in a city – a sound of church bells in London, an urban rumour in Dublin – as they walked around. Joyce's *Ulysses* and and Virginia Woolf's *Mrs Dalloway* were written at a time when the guide was a regimental dispatch rider on the Western Front or else the fomenter of a putsch in Munich and the architect was a child of the haute bourgeoisie of Mannheim courting a young woman named Margret.

It is a truism, a simplification, a popularized image, a reverie which has nothing to do with good or bad taste, but it turns out to be luminous; it has no spatial-temporal border, it is cosmopolitan, a citizen of all eras yet stateless like Albert Einstein, it crosses all nations and gathers them under the rule of the simultaneous experience of the best and the worst according to point of view and situation.

On the night of 9–10 November 1938, an architect at the top of the regime was surveying the charred ruins of the Berlin synagogue from his sleek Mercedes while an anonymous German citizen of the Jewish faith was being immolated during the 'Night of Broken Glass'. The fact that they are both in the same place, historically and geographically, the strong and the weak, this banal image of simultaneity, should provide a frame in which there is some sense of connection between them – but no, this isn't what happens. The intense fraternity of *Mrs Dalloway* and *Ulysses* is absent here. People read them – those who cared to read them – as self-enclosed, with watertight borders (until the tanks broke through). They were life-affirming novels written in periods of suffering, a symmetry, or a strange asymmetry, with neither purpose nor reason

When society is in crisis, literature thrives; when society is in crisis, literature suffers; when society is thriving, literature is in crisis; when society is thriving, so is literature: these combinations could be used to designate any period and all the fictions created during these periods, which they sometimes betray by romanticizing them far too much, making them lower or higher than they were, playing with the worst and the best of beings, and even their suffering does not escape the crazy, asocial, immoral and irreducible workings of art, which is capable of making an unforgettable character out of an executioner and an anonymous one out of a victim.

In the first half of the twentieth century, literature thrived, it was experimental, inventive, and the West underwent an unprecedented crisis, involving two global wars. We know today that for those in the South, in Africa in particular, this crisis was a blessing from Allah. It finally loosened the grip of the occupying powers, the French, the British, the Belgians, the Germans as well as the Portuguese and Italians. History is written differently according to where you are. And according to the various protagonists' situations, their lives were in crisis or they were thriving.

October 1933. The young architect became part of the Führer's inner circle, and on the 31st of that month, the Austro-Hungarian, Jewish, monarchist musician Arnold Schoenberg, an admirer of the Habsburgs, set foot in New York. He had fled the pogroms, fled the Nazis, in good time. Soon a special room in the exhibition of degenerate music in Germany would be dedicated to him, to his atonality, his dodecaphony, the twelve notes of a chromatic scale, twelve tribes of sound that formed almost infinitely divergent combinations, a metaphor for Judaism and the musical avant-garde, a reverie, one that had nothing to do with good or bad taste. Had the young music-loving architect, a friend of Wilhelm Furtwängler and Herbert von Karajan, ever listened to Arnold Schoenberg, the major and most celebrated musician of his time, whom he must have known at least by name, having seen an entire room at the exhibition of degenerate music in Düsseldorf in May 1938 dedicated to him?

April 1945. While Arnold Schoenberg was in California, advising the winner of the 1929 Nobel Prize in Literature Thomas Mann on his novel *Doctor Faustus*, the story of a brilliant German musician who made a pact with the Devil, a metaphor for Germany making a pact with Hitler, the architect and minister of armaments Albert Speer organized the last concert in Berlin. The programme included Beethoven's Violin Concerto, Bruckner's 'Romantic' Symphony No. 4, and Wagner's *Götterdämmerung* as its finale. This iconic image of the fall of Nazism as portrayed by an apocalyptic orchestra was his creation. 'When they play the "Romantic" Symphony,' he would tell his own circle of intimates, 'the end will be nigh.'

August 1947. In the Brentwood suburb of Los Angeles, Arnold Schoenberg composed *A Survivor from Warsaw* in a matter of days. It was a work for a male-voice choir and orchestra, inspired by the horrors that had taken place in Europe. It begins with a spoken song, the voice of a man trying to tell what he has experienced; he speaks and sings in English, and his memories are interspersed with orders in German, a sergeant ordering silence and a roll call; he wants to know how many there are, he sends them to the gas chamber and he must know how many there are, he beats them, and it all ends in Hebrew, the group of victims suddenly intoning, *Shem'a Yisroel, listen to Israel! The Lord our God is the only Lord. You shall love the Lord your God with all your heart, with all your soul and with all your strength. And the Commandments that I give you today shall be in your heart. You will teach them to your children and you will talk about them when you are at home, when you go on a journey, when you go to bed and when you rise.*

August 1947. Albert Speer was no longer either an architect or a minister. He was prisoner number five of seven incarcerated at Spandau, to the west of Berlin. They had been transferred from Nuremberg a month earlier. In the previous year, the seven had been given sentences ranging between ten years and life imprisonment. There had been twenty-four accused in total. Three had been discharged. The others had been sentenced to death and hanged. A few had taken their own lives before being tried. Göring had been sentenced to death and committed suicide. Bormann, who had disappeared in the closing days of the Reich, had been sentenced to death in absentia. The trials had taken place in Nuremberg, the town where he, prisoner number five, had designed rallies during the 1930s, before the catastrophe, an eternity ago. Everyone had praised his neoclassical brio and inventiveness, his anti-aircraft searchlights creating columns of light and all those banners, swastika-printed fabrics animated by the wind. He had been the architect, the guide's own artistic 'genius', which he liked to think of in terms of Pope Julius II discovering his 'divine' Michelangelo.

It was other beams of light, horizontal this time rather than vertical, cast by film projectors, which had revealed to all at the trials the particular, hitherto unseen nature of the crimes of the National Socialist regime. Film footage and testimonies from the executioners and the very rare survivors had demonstrated to everyone, and the defendants themselves, what they had ordered, in one way or another. Mostly, they had not been directly involved in the gassing of the Jews of Europe or the mass shootings in Ukraine, Belarus, Russia and the Baltic states during Operation Barbarossa. Perhaps only a handful had been on those VIP visits to certain camps without ever straying from the route designed to protect their delicate eyes. For them, all this had been merely words on paper bearing the label 'Secret', diatribes against the Jews and paragraphs in files, some orders among many employing euphemisms, and since they hadn't pulled the trigger themselves, or dropped the gas pellets down the chimneys, or participated in medical experiments on the deported, or starved the prisoners, or separated children from parents, women from men, the reserved workers from those for immediate torture, they had declared that they had been horrified by what they saw and completely dissociated themselves from the leaders of the camps or extermination squads whom they had known very well a few months earlier and whom they didn't want to know any more.

They had claimed they hadn't known, and prisoner number

five had also said he hadn't known but that it made no difference. He had said that as a leading figure in the regime, he assumed complete responsibility. It didn't matter that as an individual he was not a cog in this monstrosity, nor even that he had been unaware. As he had been a dignitary and collaborator of Adolf Hitler, collective responsibility superseded individual innocence.

He had pleaded not guilty in an individual capacity, guilty in a collective capacity.

He had impressed the jury, except for the Soviets and one American. His refusal to carry out Hitler's orders in the last months of the war had earned him a certain respect on their part. Of all the accused, he had come across as the most lucid, the most aware of what he was accused of, and his arguments had been quite convincing.

He had been arraigned on four charges: conspiracy, crimes against peace, war crimes and crimes against humanity.

He had been found guilty of the last two, the most serious ones.

His first deputy, with special responsibility for forced workers, Jewish slaves, prisoners of war or Resistance fighters from all over Europe, had been sentenced to death by hanging.

He, his chief, his Führer, had been sentenced to twenty years in prison. Intellectually and physically, he was head and shoulders above his uncouth, overweight deputy with his ridiculous, Hitler-style moustache.

Following some optimistic comments by his lawyer, he had hoped for four or five years in prison. It was all very well surviving the trial, he had told himself, but by 1966 he would be sixty-one. He would be an old man.

48

Spandau, 20 December 1947

The prisoner noted down his former life on sheets of toilet paper. Apart from one letter a month to their families, for which they were given a single sheet of paper, the inmates were not allowed to write at all. The prisoner used paper packaging and this never-ending supply of bog roll. A bit like the Marquis de Sade. He never thought about the Marquis de Sade locked up in the Bastille, composing his books, especially *The 120 Days of Sodom*, on a scroll without his jailers knowing it. He wasn't a writer, he was a war criminal and criminal against humanity, an ex-architect and an ex-minister of armaments and war production of a regime now considered to be among the worst, if not the worst, that history had ever known, and he had survived his trial. Now he was serving his sentence, writing down his memories as they came, between anxiety attacks and bouts of guilt, gardening, walking, self-pity, bad prison food and phantasmatic night-time visitations.

The guide was still there. The guide unexpectedly visited him in between conversations with the six other prisoners, who had also known him well, but not like he had, prisoner number five, his favourite.

He visited him in his cell as his hand described this monster with delicate penstrokes, so as not to tear the toilet paper. He visited him in his dreams.

You Are the Führer's Unrequited Love

He wanted to write the biography of this Hitler, as he now called him with the benefit of distance, to illuminate his own and that of the German people. He wanted to understand. He felt dazed, missing some essential but unhealthy substance, something which had revealed him to himself, from his rise to his fall, from intoxication to guilt, from exaltation to disgust, a gamut of emotion that never passed through neutral, always excessive, unbearable, incomprehensible, even now.

It was power that he was missing. As one of the defeated, he was trying to find his place in the world after Adolf Hitler. The other six talked about their Führer and insisted that his voice and the fascination he exerted on them and the crowds explained their bewitchment, shamelessly summoning up the romantic cliché of Faust and Mephistopheles, which he, the prisoner, found too simplistic, though, when push came to shove, he couldn't do much better.

The prisoner didn't think about this Hitler's voice any more. He simply homed in on his silent presence and his gaze. And suddenly the guide was there, in front of him, as before.

He enlisted in the SA at the Palace of Sports in Berlin in the spring of 1931. The prisoner had only recently joined the Party. Since he owned his own car, he became a member of the motorized section. He sometimes served as a driver for his superiors. The Berlin SA had rebelled under the influence of their local leader, an obscure nationalist who had demanded more social revolution, and the guide had dismissed this leader because he needed big business on board for his rearmament projects, and he had gathered them together in this great room to explain himself. He kept them waiting for hours, sowing anxiety, nervousness, frustration, uncertainty, and then he arrived in silence, except for the clip of his boots on the floor. He didn't mount the stage, as they had all been expecting. Instead, he suddenly veered off from the central gangway into one of the side alleys formed by the labyrinthine blocks of standing men. And he walked past them one by one, for hours, not saying a word, staring at each of them individually. And when he arrived in front of this tall, slim man he observed him for a moment the same way as he had the others. That was the first time that the prisoner had seen him close up. It was really the first time between them.

Years later, the prisoner became the guide's favourite architect, and time had already done its work: they had a shared memory filled with domes, triumphal arches and repetitive nights discoursing on the same subjects while listening to the same operettas such as *Die Fledermaus* or *The Merry Widow*, and the prisoner reminded him of that episode, certain that the other must have forgotten his face, one among thousands that day. But the guide had forgotten nothing.

'I know,' he said, 'I remember you very well!'

The Merry Widower

(1947–1980)

49

Heidelberg, Federal Republic of Germany, spring 1978

'Yes . . . It's dangerous, isn't it, to say anything positive about the men of that period. Because it is always taken as admiration or approval.'

He smiled at the woman sat in front of him as he said these words. It was a smile she was beginning to know well, in which she perceived a melancholy mixed with a certain fierce joy when he asserted how profoundly ambiguous the world and its people were. They had just been talking about Goebbels, his flaws and his qualities. 'We might even end up liking him,' she said, raising a smile from her host and setting off his screed. He made it clear that, no, Goebbels was not likeable, it was just that he had a certain talent that he put at the service of evil.

Her name was Gitta Sereny. She had come to Heidelberg to write an article about the famous Albert Speer for the *Sunday Times*. A historian and a journalist, she was Viennese by birth, and after spells in France and America she now lived in London with her husband, an American photographer called Don Honeyman.

None of her journeys had been planned. Her movements across Europe had been driven by history and its wars. Her father was a Hungarian Protestant, her mother a German Jew. According to the law – rabbinic law as much as Gentile law, and especially the law of the Nazis – that made her a Jew. At the time, she wouldn't really have thought of herself that way. Her mother was not a practising Jew, she herself went to a Protestant school. She would go to St Stephen's Cathedral almost every day, captivated by the beauty of the place. She loved Vienna and led a life of privilege, even though her father had died when she was just four years old.

She could very clearly remember March 1938, when it all came to an end. She was seventeen on the thirteenth of the month, the day after Chancellor Hitler's troops entered her country, greeted enthusiastically by the local populace. She could clearly remember the annexation of Austria by this new Germany and her best friend's mysterious request to meet up in the park that same evening. She could remember her friend's tears. Her parents had just revealed to her that they had been Nazis for years, and that this 'Anschluss', this 'connection', was a blessing, and she must no longer talk to Jews. In any case, they would all soon be exterminated, she had been told. In the park, they could hear people shouting, 'Germany awake! Death to the Jews!'

A few days later, while out for a walk, she witnessed an act of persecution. Surrounded by a jubilant crowd, a group of men and women were cleaning the pavements using toothbrushes, under the control of young Nazis in ill-assorted uniforms similar to the local SA. From Vienna to Linz, Jews had taken their own lives, others fled if they could, and these ones had been rounded up to scrub the pavements of the former capital of the Habsburg Empire. The historian clearly remembered that one of the men on their knees was her family doctor, Dr Berggrün, an eminent paediatrician. He was a Jew, as was the historian herself, via her mother, but hardly anyone knew that, and she bore her father's name. She could easily pass as a German-speaking Protestant, a Hungarian or Austrian German. She and her friend intervened against the young men of the SA. The men yelled at them. Her friend was very beautiful, the historian recalled. The Austrian SA were less experienced than their German counterparts, so all they did was yell at them and in the end they gave up. Looking back, the historian was convinced that her friend's beauty had played a role in making them back down. Young men facing a beautiful and determined young woman, young men intimidated despite their aptitude for yelling. This was three years before 1941, and they had not yet experienced naked young women holding their children in their arms, taking them to pits dug by their husbands, fathers or brothers, now executed, killed in turn by a bullet or left injured before being buried alive. The historian and her friend had intervened, the SA men had walked away, whistling, and Dr Berggrün told them off for taking such a risk. The historian would learn later that he was gassed in the extermination camp at Sobibor.

They had experienced the same events in the same places, and her memories were totally different from his. Speer had not seen or heard anything like this during his time in Vienna in the wake of the 'Anschluss'. He had only seen and heard the indescribable and totally spontaneous joy of the crowd around him as the columns of the Wehrmacht marched past, quickly shouldering their arms at the triumphal fanfares. He was the intimate friend of the most photographed man of the time, the guide's chief architect, the builder of the new Chancellery then in construction, the planner of the new Berlin. The international press had recognized him as the artist of the Nazi display at Nuremberg, with its torches and pennants interspersed with ethereal columns, using the clouds to create the most politically romantic dome in history. His old friend Leni Riefenstahl had amplified his work on celluloid. In Vienna he had thoughts only for the Ring, which so obsessed the guide and which served as a loose model for the ceremonial avenue of the Reich capital. He lived in the wake of this Führer who was adulated by the German masses and certain foreign observers, this Adolf Hitler whose name he now spat out with disgust, as indeed he still did. He was still living in the wake of that man.

He had been his number one architect. He had been his minister of armaments, a possible number two in the regime, the successor that the military and the industrialists all wanted. He had been prisoner number five at Spandau. He was now catnip for historians and the media.

When he had left Spandau prison, at the stroke of midnight on 1 October 1966, a crowd of journalists was waiting for him and the surrounding streets were heaving with onlookers. He wasn't alone, the former head of the Hitler Youth shared his good fortune, and they had left the prison together, appearing before the people gathered there, as many if not more than would attend a film festival. And all eyes were focused on him, prisoner number five, now free. The attention had never let up since. He had really become the star Riefenstahl had spotted when she cut his picture out of a magazine.

50

The first time that the historian saw the star was at his trial in Nuremberg. She knew nothing about him. She was struck by this tall, slim man, still young-looking, a distinguished forty-year-old, the polar opposite of the vulgar idiots arraigned alongside him, whom he greeted courteously, just as he was extremely attentive and respectful throughout the whole procedure towards the judges, lawyers, executioners and victims who had come to testify to the horrors of the regime. He was not at all like Göring and the rest, he was their exact counterpoint. Some physiques more than others are the vessels of personality, they play more easily than others the role of orchestra soloist, and they do so for many reasons. They are to do with the criteria of beauty of a given culture, the injustice of forms in nature which means that a cat is more likely to appear on a coat of arms than a cockroach, a tarantula or a water-boatman; they are to do with how good or not a face looks. Advertisers know this, propagandists know it, everyone knows it, and in the eyes of the young historian as of the judges, the one she was observing was more of a wise lion than his fellow prisoners. Göring, sober, free of make-up, fingernails and toenails unpainted, did his bling-bling thing, standing up to speak when not invited to, being sarcastic and confrontational with the judges, while the others looked bored, fidgeting in their seats, and some of them just seemed crazy, like Rudolf Hess, the former secretary of the Reich Chancellery.

Not the star.

The historian was twenty-four, she had been invited to the trial by one of her translator friends, and of all the accused it was Albert Speer that she remembered most, his immobility, his demeanour, his complete self-possession, his gaze, in which she read intelligence, concentration and a few things besides that she was unable to put a name to; he was a someone endowed with a certain charisma. A handsome man, for sure. And like most of the public, the judges and journalists, the translators and secretaries, she had one question on her mind. She wondered how a man such as this could associate himself with the bunch of mediocrities around him. In his gaze she also noticed something that she termed 'dark'. She didn't know whether that really came from him or whether all the horrors of the regime that she was hearing about and seeing haloed him in this dark glow that she attributed to his eyes.

She didn't hear his voice, she came only three times and never saw him take the witness stand; he had remained in his seat, sculptural and concentrated. She first heard it years later after his release from Spandau, when he popped up everywhere, invited onto radio and TV in Germany, and even in London, where the BBC were very keen on him. He talked about Hitler, Nazism, the camps and himself. She listened to him and found it all highly unpleasant, this mix of facile charm and glibly worn guilt, and yet she couldn't bring herself to conclude that he was manipulative.

Nevertheless, she thought Albert Speer's situation was extraordinary. She was not the only one to think that; her colleagues in the media, publishing houses, universities or simply the wider public shared this feeling, which was created by this man's cold demeanour, his self-confidence, even when coming across as humble and ashamed of the past, of his blindness and deafness when he was the architect, the minister, the favourite of Adolf Hitler. That he could have been all that and at the same time now find himself sitting peacefully in front of BBC microphones is a fact beyond the scope of his story, it makes him into a character from the Marquis de Sade, living proof that in this world vice prospers and virtue fails. The truism that injustice is the underlying law of nature no longer holds up with him, the favourite, the architect, Hitler's minister who gained his stardom for these very reasons. The historian mused on the fact that no survivor of the Holocaust possessed such an aura for both the masses and the specialists. Elie Wiesel or Simon Wiesenthal, perhaps, but their fame was no match for that of the star Albert Speer.

Of course, theirs was respectable whereas the star's was disreputable, and he never baulked at replying to those who reminded him of that in more or less veiled terms in radio or television interviews. But in general, it all went well for him, just as it had, basically, since the start of his life. He had been born into a well-off family. He hadn't been beaten or abused by his parents or by other adults or friends. He had done well at school. He had built monuments. He had held prestigious posts. He was now much sought-after. Those twenty years of incarceration had been his only encounter with misfortune. But he had transformed his prison experience into a spiritual experience, reading more than 5,000 books, exploring his culpability as a German in relation to the extermination of the Jews.

He had become an incomparable object of interest in the eyes of the world, and since leaving Spandau he himself had contributed to the making of his image through two books that became bestsellers. The historian had read them and found them fascinating, totally irresistible.

First, *Inside the Third Reich*, the memoirs going from his birth up to the trial at Nuremberg, essentially devoted to his relationship with Hitler. It is a fantastical gallery of portraits, of first-hand accounts that now provide raw material for films and history textbooks, feeding both the search for historical truth on the part of some and the fictional creations of others through spectacular scenes such as those during the famous, almost mythical last days of the Third Reich.

Then, *Spandau Diaries*, his prison journal. From extracts at least, particularly those re-edited at the time of their publication, she knew it well. Here the historian found an even more interesting figure: fragile, fissured, seeking to become a different man. She followed his hopes and his despair, his sadness at not seeing his children grow up, the visitations of Hitler in his sleep, his insomnia, his mental tortures, his work as gardener, his reading of philosophical and religious texts, especially of the Protestant theologian Karl Barth, whose five-volume *Church Dogmatics* he studied in detail. In spite of the restrictions, he received newspapers, the guards kept him informed, the prisoners discussed things between them, and she was able to observe him, the former man of power, become a spectator of a new world where he could no longer do anything or decide anything.

She learned of his friendship with his Protestant confessor, a Frenchman and former member of the Resistance called Georges Casalis. She was amazed at what she discovered, like when he decided to convert his daily walk in the prison yard into a journey around the world. To her this was a remarkable, utterly cosmopolitan *Wanderweg*, the most beautiful travel story imaginable, because here to travel really was to escape, to

You Are the Führer's Unrequited Love

transform a single place into a world tour, the names of foreign cities evoking a sincere yearning for elsewhere. A walk around the world. Starting on 30 September 1954, he began to note down how many kilometres he had covered. First he wanted to go to Heidelberg, back to the house of his parents where his wife and children now lived. That was 626 kilometres. He loved these elementary calculations, the magic of numbers, their entirely natural power, from zero to infinity, at least to Heidelberg in the first instance. He calculated the length of his steps, using the sole of his shoe as a unit of measurement. In one month, he had walked 240 kilometres. For him, a man of action, this imaginary tour of the world was all he was able to do. The historian followed him during his peregrinations. Vienna, Belgrade, Budapest, Sofia, Istanbul, then the Middle East, the Far East. He headed eastward. He remembered the preludes of Liszt and 22 June 1941, when the army bore down on the Soviet Union. *Drang nach Osten*, the 'march on the East', a geopolitical expression dear to romantic and nationalist German culture, the great and beautiful German culture that was much broader than Nazism. He remembered his brother, missing in action at Stalingrad in late 1942 or early 1943. On 13 July 1959, he arrived in Beijing. He imagined all the adventures and political complications he would face. Deep down, the historian found him more of an artist than ever, in the most normal sense of the term, a man capable of revelatory fantasies. On 30 September 1966, the last day of his incarceration, he was in the vicinity of Guadalajara in Mexico. He asked one of his friends to come and fetch him there, that night, when the gates of Spandau would open. He amused himself. He was moved. He was free, he had corresponded with Karl Barth and others, he had aroused compassion in a number of people, including some victims of the National Socialist regime. He had written on more than 20,000 sheets of toilet paper enough material for several books and he had almost walked around the world, more than 31,936 kilometres.

The historian finished these books convinced by the writer, but doubting the man she encountered on the radio and the television, a contradictory response that both troubled her and inspired her at the same time.

51

Their first exchanges were in the form of letters. The star wrote to the historian in July 1977 concerning an article of hers that he had read in the *Sunday Times*, in which she had debunked the claims of a British denialist who had argued that Hitler knew nothing about the extermination of the Jews. He congratulated her and said it was absurd to claim such a thing, nothing of any importance in the Reich would have taken place without a decision from Hitler. He described these attempts at denialism as 'grotesque'. He said that he was 'appalled'.

The very next day, she received a second letter, in which he told her that he had read her book *Into the Darkness*, an account of the commandant of the Treblinka death camp based on interviews and reflections. The star asked her if she would like to meet him one day, perhaps at his house in Heidelberg? He gave her his telephone number.

The historian's life was built around executioners and their victims. They had become her speciality, her ongoing passion. She lived with them from morning until night.

After the annexation of Austria, she had fled to Switzerland, then to France, where she became involved in the Resistance during the Occupation. She took care of children who had been lost or abandoned due to the war. The setting was idyllic, the chateau of Villandry next to the Loire, whose owner had taken them in and offered them protection. German soldiers often visited the chateau, and she particularly remembered two of them who took an interest in the welfare of the orphans. The historian had regarded these two as no better than their comrades. They wore the same uniform, and that was that. She had unrelentingly despised them, hated them, and now she felt somewhat ashamed. She learned some years afterwards that they had disapproved of the regime because of their Christian beliefs. They tried wherever possible to mitigate the suffering caused by their side. One day, they suddenly weren't there any more – one sent to the Russian front, the other to a concentration camp.

Later on, an officer of the same ilk even saved her life. She had hidden a British pilot. The Gestapo found out and were going to arrest her. He warned her, gave her some money and put her on a train to Paris, from where she could be exfiltrated to America.

Since then, she resisted coming to snap judgements about people and occupied what is known as the grey zone. She studied the case of Mary Flora Bell, a British Lolita aged eleven who had killed two little boys aged four and three. She reported on child prostitution in America and Europe. She wrote about the commandant of Treblinka. She was very familiar with that grey zone; she would often hear interviewees, especially former Nazis, insist that nothing was completely black or white but, on the contrary, everything was more or less grey. It was the zone generally inhabited by the executioners and their inner circles, people responsible for atrocities, she was aware of that. It included some victims too, which was even more disturbing. Not to mention that, with the ascendancy of the human sciences, particularly sociology, psychology and psychoanalysis, causality was key; if an executioner turned out to be a former victim, this was considered a valid reason for their actions. She subscribed to this twentieth-century view of things, and yet, now and then, she allowed herself a less rational uncertainty about questions of good and evil, an uncertainty that no explanation could diminish, quite the opposite.

It was by listening to broadcasts and especially by reading articles attacking the star that she realized the kind of fury he aroused. It was this fury that impassioned her. It reminded her of her own against those two Christian German officers. The anger against Speer in the end outweighed all the arguments, the anger of seeing this man peacefully living off his bestsellers and his past in the service of Hitler. Sure, he had been tried and sentenced to twenty years in prison, he had done his time according to the rules laid down by the victors themselves, and yet it still seemed as if destiny were laughing in the face of the millions of victims who had suffered under the most awful circumstances by making him first Hitler's special one and now a star of the historians and the media.

The evening after she received the second letter, the historian phoned him. His voice was another surprise to her. It was very hesitant, questioning. He seemed in need of reassurance, or else he was being excessively cautious. He was very different from the public figure that she had heard on television and the radio.

She had spoken to a number of Nazis, but never one so close to Hitler. She was perfectly aware that this was the voice that had spoken daily with the dictator, shared the dreams and feelings that the latter reserved exclusively for this tall, slim young man, the archetypal Aryan that he vaunted in his speeches. She was aware of the anomaly that he was still there when so many people had died, but before actually speaking to him, these had all been theoretical notions. A fascinating subject, of course, but distant and abstract. Now he was speaking to her directly. She was conversing with the man who had been at the heart of a regime considered to be the epitome of Evil on Earth and had occupied a unique place thanks to his special relationship with Hitler, and he was still alive and was just asking to talk about it, again and again.

Over the next few months they kept in touch, sharing things they had read, sending each other books and newspaper articles in both German and English. She was increasingly assailed by contradictory emotions. One day, she proposed writing an article with him about his 'case' for the *Sunday Times Magazine*. He accepted. The historian and her husband made the journey from London to Heidelberg. They had agreed to stay there for about three weeks.

The Second World War had finished thirty-three years earlier, and the number of survivors of the camps willing to bear witness was dwindling; the hunt for exfiltrated Nazis was becoming more hit and miss; young people born after the war were wearing swastikas as badges; it was a truism, but the world was changing; perceptions of the past were different in the younger generation; Holocaust denial was becoming more common; there was more indifference, more provocation; a certain weariness and retrospective fascination crept into conversations and magazine articles, and as far as the 1933–1945 period was concerned, historians faced a greater struggle against alternative interpretations, denials and provocations.

But this didn't matter, it was now the historians' moment, and for Sereny the star was a prey not to be missed.

52

Fucking traitor:

We've been looking for you for a long time. When you were our Führer's architect you gained so much from him when he achieved victory after victory. Then you planned to gas him and his staff when he was defending our Berlin . . . etc.

It was the morning of their first day together, and the historian was reading this threatening, insulting letter that the star had received. One among many. She would record it verbatim and reproduce it in a biography that she would write about him one day.

The star seemed almost proud of it. This type of letter proved that he had disassociated himself from the past, that he had become the enemy of Nazis present and past, those of them that remained, whom he had known well and who no longer talked to him. Minor figures, it had to be said, third-class functionaries who, at least until his books and his media commentaries, had always regarded him as their Führer's favourite, the wunderkind minister of armaments of the now defunct Reich. Simple groupies, all the more ridiculous now in defeat. There is nothing more pathetic than the defeated, and he wasn't one of that mob, at least not in that way. He had been defeated, but he had raised himself up through the courageous way he had assumed guilt in the eyes of the world, whereas his former comrades . . . He pitied them and deep down despised these subordinates whom the guide and his circle regarded with their paternalistic authority as mere pawns on their chessboard. They were ex-Nazis who disapproved of the gas chambers but not of Hitler, a man who had saved their country from humiliation and bankruptcy in 1933 and whom they had difficulty connecting with the crematoria of Auschwitz, that is when they didn't simply deny their existence. In the late 1970s, they still constituted the vast majority of the German population over forty. This majority kept silent, not wishing to raise the subject, but that didn't mean they didn't think about it.

The star knew this well. He was the one who, by assuming the collective guilt for the crimes that some of them had committed, had played a role in raising the nation's awareness of these crimes. That is how he saw himself, and he was happy that younger people seemed to judge him more favourably than the members of his own generation and shared his point of view. They were constantly interrogating their elders about their past. He was ahead of his time and he loved these young people in particular, their invigorating presence, full of new, athletic blood, the very epitome of the vital force. He had played this role, and it was a political as much as a moral one. He still knew how to play a political role, even if it was restricted to the moral dimension. Sometimes he confessed a nostalgia for when he was at the heart of things, that unbeatable excitement of power.

He had met the historian the previous evening, and they had dined together for the first time. She was staying with him, which made it easier to talk. She didn't want to interrogate him. She wanted a dialogue. His replies would emerge from their exchanges. The silences would be as eloquent as the words themselves. Nevertheless, she had some questions that she wanted to ask. Obviously. She wouldn't ask them directly. She made written notes, she didn't film. She didn't need to worm information out of him simply to make good footage. Cinema is always a bit totalitarian on this point, the camera shoved in your face, the instructions from the director, the expectation. It is like the eye of a policeman. They followed this daily routine over the course of several weeks.

The star and Margret, his wife, were seventy-three. He looked as tall and slim as before. Perhaps only a slight stoop. His bushy eyebrows had not turned white, but his hair had, and it had receded from his forehead. The fringe which he once elegantly combed to one side was no longer there. He had aged well, and his author royalties kept him in comfort, not to mention the invitations to speak about Hitler and his inner circle on TV or radio and the publishing tours that come with being a successful author, that admit you to a certain well-educated, liberal European culture, yet another paradox for this former Nazi leader and an insane injustice for many of his detractors.

He was a man of an older generation who maintained an extremely courteous distance with women. As he had never been a lothario and had always been faithful to his wife, this courteous distance was even more eloquent. The historian experienced it at first hand. Conversely, he was always more at ease with Don, her photographer husband, with whom he was very quickly on first-name terms.

Don was meant to take a few photographs of the star and then make himself scarce, leaving him alone with the historian, and the star made a joke about this. 'I won't have Don here to protect me from you,' he joshed.

He was evidently unafraid of those present and past Nazis and their threatening letters. The name A. SPEER was written in enormous letters on one of the pillars of his gateway. It was like a commemorative plaque. The historian complimented him on his nice house. The star shot back, in a strange voice, that he, in fact, detested it. It was his childhood home, and he was surprisingly vehement in his hatred. Margret demurred somewhat; she also thought it was a nice house, she had lived there with her children during his incarceration in Spandau, but he got worked up again and went on venting his animus towards the building. She was a woman of an older generation, she tended not to stand up to her husband, so after her slight demurral, a single discordant note in his angry solo, she shut up and let him carry on.

The star was a man with a very specific form of intelligence, the political and radical type, which had come into its own when tested by total war at the heart of a regime that was itself very particular, with its unprecedented mixture of racism and aestheticism, which provoked the excitement of the masses, the murderous imperial pride of the masses that had never shown itself before, sacrificing whole peoples to the cult of blood and soil. The historian found it very difficult to distinguish where cold calculation started and finished with this man, whether he was resorting to the clichés of an unhappy childhood to play to his audience or whether he really did feel some distress in relation to the little boy he once was, deprived of love by his parents. The specific intelligence of this man was not simply subordinated to the regime. It *was* that regime, one of its strongest facets, and it was very difficult for the historian, now sitting in front of him in the dining room of his house in Heidelberg, to know whether, even when discussing the most banal biographical facts of his childhood, he was still applying those strategic and tactical skills he had employed with the members of Hitler's inner circle in order to climb the Nazi greasy pole.

After all, he was an authentic man of power and of images, and what power did he have left other than the power to create a final image of himself, that of a moral figure who had lived

You Are the Führer's Unrequited Love

through absolute amorality, a moral figure who had escaped from the most extreme art and politics of his century and perhaps of all time? She didn't know, but she was here to find out.

The historian set out her stall at this very first dinner. She had read his books and everything she could find about him. She knew all his arguments, all his defence mechanisms. For of course, since his bestsellers had been published, some historians had begun to question his version of events, so he must have sharpened up his blunted defences since Nuremberg.

He nodded, he understood perfectly. He knew it, though he had hoped for something else. He was disappointed, he seemed genuinely disappointed. She was just like the others, he told her wearily. She wanted what everyone called 'the truth' on *that* topic. They all had the same question in their minds, every time, and she was no different. 'You are like the others,' he repeated to her during dinner. 'You have this question in your head. Why not ask it now and have done with it?'

That question was the one about the Jews, the extermination of the Jews.

That question was how could a man of his rank make out that he knew nothing about what happened to the Jews? How could the minister of armaments and the war economy, who had millions of slaves at his disposal, including many Jews, claim that he knew nothing?

No, it was an even more precise question than that. The question was: did he know the means by which the Jews were murdered? Did he know about Treblinka, Auschwitz and other death camps?

So why not ask him this question about the Jews straight away and be done with it?

53

Over the course of three weeks, they revisited all the major events of his life one by one. She had him give an oral account of what he had written in his books and said in interviews, watching out for any contradictions.

At one point they left Heidelberg and went to a house in the Bavarian mountains that he had bought and comfortably furnished with his author royalties. They skied and went walking in the spring snowdrifts of the Bavarian Alps.

The historian found the experience head-spinning.

The architect had walked with Hitler in the Bavarian Alps, and now she was walking with him in the same manner in the same place, listening to him as he had listened to his Führer.

He had experienced the seductive power of Hitler, she in turn was experiencing the seductive power of this man.

He talked about Hitler's charisma, now she could talk about the undeniable charisma of his favourite.

He had been Hitler's architect, now she was becoming Albert Speer's historian.

She wasn't seeking to glorify herself by building a Chancellery on paper; rather, she was trying to uncover the truth about his accountability. Nevertheless, every incriminating or exculpatory remark reinforced his legend, for good or ill. He was a monumental figure, his name existed in a place where otherwise there was merely an anonymous number, a quantity versus a personality, six million Jews and millions of other victims of forced labour in the wartime factories versus Albert Speer, the only member of Hitler's inner circle to enjoy his liberty, the cameras and all the attention.

And like the architect with the guide, the historian and the star had almost formed a friendship, far exceeding their purely professional relationship. She avowed that he was a handsome man, but there was never any physical attraction between them. At some point she mentioned that he had touched her shoulder one evening when he came to her room to share his wife's fears about an impending interview on the Jewish question, but that was all. She had promised him then that she would never speak about the Jews to Margret, and while he was thanking her, she had the sensation of him brushing her with his hand, just as the star had described Hitler doing somewhere in his memoirs.

It was a dizzying, distressing, exhilarating, excruciating situation, a set of discordant feelings based on the parallels between the architect and the guide on the one hand and the historian and the star on the other.

One day, she spoke to him about a speculative article by a psychoanalyst on the nature of his relationship with Hitler. No question of anything sexual between them – they wouldn't have been capable of that – but something the author characterized as homoeroticism, an irresistible mutual attraction for their respective statuses as artist and man of power, former combatant and slim young man, the only relationship possible between these two men who were so inhibited that gleeful commentators would make heavy, unsubtle hints about Hitler's supposed anatomy and sexuality.

The star listened attentively to this and admitted that the

psychoanalyst was very close to the truth. They had one of those eminently masculine relationships that no woman could ever match.

The question of the Jews and what he did or didn't know was perhaps no longer the sole reason for her visit.

54

Sometimes, with much reluctance and apprehension, the historian pondered whether Hitler's unprecedented antisemitism might be the cover for something else, without being able to put her finger on what that something else was. Perhaps she was looking to Speer to give a name to this thing? Most of the time, however, she refrained from going down that route, where reason ends and metaphysics begins, and evil is no longer about morality or legality, but the domain of the Devil and his foul works. That would be to lapse into Faustian folklore and succumb to that infantilizing fascination for the Nazi period that she had observed among the youth of the 1970s.

The historian and the star read the papers and watched the television news. They were both of that generation that saw reading the main dailies and magazines as essential: television was no substitute, merely a supplement to it. They scoured the papers every day and afforded them an intellectual respect that no longer exists today. To them, they were still the bastions of analysis and debate, of film and book reviews, or forums and investigations researched in greater or lesser detail according to talents and means, as well as informing them about the changes in fashion, and the recent developments in youth culture and the arts, rock, pop, the hippy movement and what the British were now calling punk.

Like everyone in the course of the 1960s and 1970s, the star and the historian had come across photos of a certain Brian Jones, member of a famous rock band, posing in an SS uniform, and the record sleeve of another group of the same genre, the Beatles, portraying Adolf Hitler alongside poets, actresses and scientists such as Marilyn Monroe and Albert Einstein. They had noticed swastikas on T-shirts, necklaces and kids' jackets. Nazism had become a facile symbol of absolute evil, and was attractive to certain young people for precisely that reason. Unfortunately, this was not so different from the historian's hypothesis that Hitler's unprecedented antisemitism was a cover for something else. These kids were not especially antisemitic; rather, they had a morbid fascination with Nazism's malevolent reputation, its diabolical character, the typically black SS uniforms, the swastikas, the raised-arm, hand-out salutes, the 'Heil Hitlers' randomly uttered by clueless teens. Provocation and transgression were now fashionable, especially in the arts, and what could be more transgressive and provocative than the Third Reich? These young people were not especially Nazi, but the symbols had their own power, some more than others.

Hitler had been transformed into a pop culture icon, and his iconography now informed numerous films, such as those of the great Italian master Luchino Visconti, and even more recent productions in West Germany, such as those of Rainer Werner Fassbinder, whose films had been making headlines. An American minimalist sculptor portrayed himself as a gay Nazi in a photo, a German artist composed monumental muddy-grey canvases with views of German ruins where he appears giving a Nazi salute, dressed in the uniform of the Wehrmacht.

The star who was sitting right next to her had made this iconography. They didn't speak about it much. They touched on the columns of light at the Nuremberg rallies. The star felt a jab of melancholic pride. He thought about the posterity of his oeuvre, troubled that there was not much of it left, not even ruins, except at Nuremberg, the ultimate remains of his work.

She shared with him that in September 1934 she was in the same place at the same time as him, at that famous rally. And that she had found it exciting and beautiful. She was thirteen at the time. She had been studying in England and was on the way home to her mother, in Vienna. Her train had broken down in Nuremberg, and while they were repairing it, to keep the children occupied, the authorities had sent them to the Zeppelin field. The horizontal lines of the steps and the stands, the geometric blocks of men on the square, the banners, the columns of light after sunset, the kids of her age from the Hitler Youth, all these things had totally seduced her, and she had joined in the acclaim as speaker after speaker mounted the rostrum at the end of the esplanade. She hadn't understood anything they were talking about, but it didn't matter. Only the drama of the event counted. She hadn't understood a thing, she was more or less ignorant of antisemitism; she had never been called a dirty Jew, and on hearing the account she later gave to her class, her teacher had given her *Mein Kampf* to read, to help her to understand what she had witnessed.

The star listened to her and nodded his head, convinced but disappointed: that's what he would be remembered for. Not for his buildings and his projects but solely for the theatre of Nuremberg, the staging, the iconography that subsequent events had rendered beyond the pale, the most toxic example of art subordinated to politics.

Nevertheless, it was the minister, not the architect, who featured most in their conversations. The favourite played a primary role. And he told the historian his story for the umpteenth time.

More than anyone, he was a man who was made up of several

layers, or more precisely several versions of himself, and the historian had to remain vigilant to tell them apart. Her aim was to find the most plausible one.

There was obviously what he had experienced.

There was what he had written about his experiences.

There was what historians and investigative journalists increasingly wrote about him, comparing his own statements with what they had been able to find in the archives.

There was what the former minor members of the inner circle had written about him in their own memoirs, which was generally deceptive, a caricature too much based on personal grievance to be credible.

There was what he had said in interviews and private conversations, like the ones he and the historian had been having these past few days, for twelve hours a day, on the things he had experienced and about which he had written, where sometimes there were some slight but disturbing differences between what he said and what he had written, which provided the subject of further improvised exegeses over a meal or on a walk.

And then there was what his former friends and colleagues might say about him off the record.

The historian hadn't met them yet. She had only seen the star and part of his family. The tension in the air when the star had his children around him was so palpable that the historian pointed it out almost immediately. He didn't shy away from it. Communication between them was difficult, displays of affection were impossible. He held himself totally responsible for that. There were six – two daughters, four sons. They had been born between 1934 and 1943. His work, the war and prison had prevented him from being with them. He hadn't seen them grow up. Their father was a stranger to them, and they to him. When they were reunited, the day after he left prison, they didn't know what to say to each other. The eldest, Albert Friedrich Speer, became an architect himself, the standard bearer of the family tradition. Hilde, the second oldest, had some meaningful correspondence with him during his detention in Spandau. She supported him the best she could. Along with her father's former secretary, and one of his best friends and closest collaborators at the time of the Berlin Bureau of Construction they became a sort of triumvirate of moral and material support, collecting funds and recovering his fragmentary memories written on toilet roll and other bits of wrapping paper.

She gave him two gifts: her filial love, despite his lack of paternal involvement in his family, and her lucidity. She interrogated him about Nazism. She didn't hold back. She asked him about his own personal responsibility. She wanted to know and to understand, just as later the children of the 1960s wanted to know and understand the exact role their parents played in this Third Reich whose atrocities filled their history books at school while at home it was as if this was ancient history concerning people other than themselves.

He was astonished at the time that his daughter could ask such questions. They forced him, for his part, to examine his conscience, which of course he had done before, but with a stranger, the French Protestant pastor Georges Casalis. This time, the demands came from his own daughter.

He had always insisted, in his interviews and writings, that it was impossible to represent the Hitler dictatorship without having lived through it, a claim that is both debatable and irrefutable. Morally, it is irrefutable, as it rests on the major yet inevitable fault of historians, novelists or anyone else interested in the past, but especially the Third Reich, namely, their retrospective judgements, their anachronisms, informed by everything that is now common knowledge about this era and the horrors it perpetrated.

But when it is the person in question himself who says this, the only character in the story to have played a major role before, during and after, and in different costumes, the claim is more debatable. Reading him, then hearing it for herself, the historian was, despite herself, sucked into this man's version of the truth. He described his Third Reich after the event, in full knowledge of the extermination of the Jews, which he claimed not to have known about at the time, with his threefold claim and its logical consequence: 'I didn't know then, I do know now, I should have known: I am therefore guilty.' But at the same time, he gave the impression that he no longer knew what he knew at the time . . . He gave this impression, and it was impossible to tell whether it was deliberate, involuntary or a little of both. More than once he consciously resorted to effects to sow this uncertainty.

He behaved in the same way with his daughter. But their correspondence brought them together; you might even say that they began to form a proper father–daughter bond from the moment they started writing to each other. At one point the star expressed concern about a study trip she was going to make to America, advising her not to say anything about her familiarity with Hitler. For she had indeed known him, she had shaken hands with him and spoken to him, and there were photos showing them together with other children at Berchtesgaden.

Despite their correspondence, Hilde didn't end up knowing much more about her father than anyone who had read his memoirs.

The historian too, at the beginning of her stay, wasn't convinced that she would learn much more. But when they parted after three weeks of intense discussion, she was certain that he had known about the Jews. She said it to his face a short time before she left.

55

Everyone asked him this question, and he understood that it was now the historian's turn. She had chosen her moment well. At the very start, in somewhat melodramatic fashion, he had urged her to come right out with this damn question about the Jews, to take the initiative, to defuse any intrigue between them, so he could give the reply that he had given to everyone else and had written in his bestsellers: collectively guilty, individually innocent.

He would have presented this argument in spite of the things that had emerged recently, which they had spoken about, that terrible article from 1971, in which an American journalist of Polish origin and camp survivor Erich Goldhagen had revealed the speech by Himmler in Posen in 1943 in which he namechecked Speer and thanked him.

'It was the biggest blow I had received since Nuremberg,' he had confided in her. To her, this showed one of his worst faults, which obscured everything else: his incredible egocentrism that made everything about him, his feelings and his suffering, and his lack of any sustained or deep empathy with his listeners. He had turned to the archives to prove that he hadn't been present the afternoon that Himmler delivered his speech and so had not been lying, that he had known nothing about these things before Nuremberg.

★

The article from a Holocaust survivor and Himmler and SS specialist had almost brought everything crashing down. Until its publication, the star had succeeded in forging a moral persona who had assumed the full collective guilt of genocidal National Socialism as one of its major leaders, even though he had not participated in the crimes directly or even known about them. It had almost been a gift of himself, a sublime gift to the German people, and an act of chivalry to the victims. Socially and financially, he had also rehabilitated himself.

When he had gone to London for the first time, at the invitation of the media, he had been briefly detained by officials who were amazed to see one of the top Nazi chiefs casually disembarking. But everything had been quickly sorted out and he had taken no offence, nor had he complained about those who passed judgement on all this scandalous notoriety. He was an undisputed master of image and iconography, he had presented himself as humble and upright in the face of his detractors, giving the unconscious impression of an eminently Christian man undergoing a sort of Passion or Calvary. Christ had assumed the sins of the world, and the star took on his shoulders all the sins of Nazism. And life was good for him again, it had never stopped being so, except in Spandau, to some extent. Even in Spandau he had managed to transform his incarceration into a monastic experience, seeking the path of true redemption with an unimpeachable honesty. This was not for show, a projection of the image he tried to maintain of himself, but an internal, thoroughgoing change such that he would never again be that Speer who was the love of Hitler to the bitter end. When he had met Georges Casalis, it was as if he had found a possible intermediary for that redemption. On hearing his first sermon, the star, who was still a prisoner, had asked him to 'help him become another man'. It had only lasted three years, the pastor had not renewed his contract, but their relationship had left an indelible mark, especially on the pastor.

To his great surprise, the star did not re-establish contact after Spandau. It was as if he had fulfilled his role, and the star had no need of him any more. As the historian discovered, this was how he behaved with everyone.

After Spandau, he had spent two years writing his memoirs, gathering together all the pieces of toilet paper scrupulously preserved by his former secretary and especially his constant friend, his former colleague at the Berlin bureau and later the ministry. The friend had supported Margret and the children like no one else and had set up a support fund for Speer and his family.

When he read the star's memoirs, he discovered that he no longer existed. Not only was he not thanked, but his name wasn't mentioned anywhere. In their exchanges, Speer explained that he hadn't wanted to compromise him, as he was pursuing a respectable career as an architect in postwar Germany and would not benefit from being linked to him, Hitler's former favourite. That is exactly what the friend found so disgusting when he read *Inside the Third Reich*. How could Speer denigrate the Führer in this way? How could he refer to him purely as a criminal, after everything Hitler had done for them, for him especially, the favourite? How could he have forgotten that special relationship, that fellow feeling that united them beyond their professional and ideological interests, which everyone commented upon with a mixture of amazement and jealousy? Didn't he know, he of all people, that there is no black and white, just grey, and that applied to the Führer too? Did he not recall that their ministry employed people who were half-Jewish, in other words Jews, thus saving them from deportation and death, like Marion Riesser, who had helped to sort through the sheets of toilet paper and transcribe them? If a half-Jew like

Marion Riesser, whose praises he had often sung, and whose grandmother had died in the Theresienstadt death camp, was so devoted to going through the papers of the Führer's ex-minister, it must mean that things weren't as black and white as his memoirs made out.

And the same thing applied to the Führer, he insisted further. The friend still sometimes wrote 'the Führer'. He didn't hate him. And the friend knew why his beloved Albert Speer had wiped their friendship from his life. He had read the different versions of his writings as well as the documents produced at the time of the ministry and the bureau, notably around the time of the expulsion of the Jews from Berlin. And if he thought that Hitler wasn't all black, he also knew his beloved Albert Speer was not all white either. And that was something his beloved Albert Speer did not want to be known.

But at the end of the day this didn't matter to the star. His memoirs were phenomenally successful, they turned him into something of a writer, and he jokingly said that he had a hundred or so books inside him, all on the Third Reich, all on Hitler and his inner circle ... and on wartime production, and on ceremonial architecture, and on the slave-worker and concentration camp system of the regime, and on how Hitler talked and behaved in private or in public, and how in the beginning there had been this contrast between the private man and the head of state, the Führer – a death trap – and all sorts of other subjects that he struggled to get out of his head, much to the dismay of his family, and particularly Margret, who, more than anyone, wanted to move on, wishing that he would once and for all stop living with *him*, their former Führer.

His love for Hitler had turned into hate and contempt, and his former friends and colleagues from that glorious period in National Socialist history, when they had dreamed up their domes and arms factories, found it hypocritical and frankly even ignoble, a betrayal, and they distanced themselves from him after the huge success of *Inside the Third Reich* in 1969. But the star didn't give a damn, new friends came along, more in keeping with the new image he had successfully created for himself.

The star showed the historian what he described as a priceless letter. It came from a certain Raphael Geis, a rabbi. Dated November 1969, the letter contained the most precious words of his life. The rabbi had told him that he hadn't yet read his memoirs, but he had seen him on television and he knew of his testimony at Nuremberg. He confessed that he didn't understand him, but that he saw in him a man who was different and honest, and as a devout Jew he regarded him now as 'walking beneath the star of forgiveness'.

The star had not hoped for such forgiveness, and the fact that it came from a rabbi completely astonished him. They became friends. For three years, up until the death of Raphael Geis, they corresponded and met up, much to the disapproval of Geis' wife and children. He had been deported to Buchenwald and miraculously released around 1939, having acquired a visa for British Palestine, where he had lived until 1952. He had witnessed the rebirth of Israel but he remained homesick for his native Germany and finally returned there. He loved the country despite its crimes.

The rabbi became for the star what the Protestant pastor had been for prisoner number five, a moral touchstone, a voice of conscience. He consulted him when he wanted to anonymously donate part of his new fortune to some Jewish organization or other, and sometimes the rabbi reproached him for doing too much.

He had once again become a member of the haute bourgeoisie in the new, post-Nazi Germany, the friend of a rabbi and of people with prodigious moral and intellectual authority, such as the theologian Karl Barth. It really was a *Vita Nova*, a redemption too, the beginning of a strange, unprecedented career in letters, both as historian of himself and as the favoured subject of professional historians, yet without any real threat to his recently acquired reputation.

And then this article by Erich Goldhagen had appeared and swept it all away.

And yet, he got away with it, and not only because of his shaky justification that he wasn't there when the grotesque Reichsführer-SS Himmler gave his speech on 3 October 1943. Why his new reputation wasn't more dented than that by Goldhagen's methodical work is unanswerable, the question remains hanging in the relationship between fiction and reality.

He was also afraid of losing his new-found friends, but that too did not transpire. Raphael Geis had been ill when the article appeared and he had simply begged the star to desist from stirring up the past and above all to lead 'a normal life, made up of a bit of calm in the present and an even more calm and contemplative life in the future'.

His rabbi friend had died shortly afterwards, but he had other friendships that were just as important.

In 1974, he had received a letter signed by Simon Wiesenthal, who was famous for tracking down Nazis holed up in South America, like Adolf Eichmann and Franz Stangl, the subject of one of the historian's books. Even though Goldhagen's article revealing Himmler's speech in Posen had appeared three years earlier, Wiesenthal asked him when and on what occasion he had first heard about the extermination of the Jews, and Speer respectfully gave him the same reply he gave to everybody: the first he had heard of it was at the Nuremberg trials. The star also expressed his admiration for his book *The Sunflower*. Here too a friendship was formed, and they began sharing their views on Hitler and other, always identical subjects – Nazism, the Holocaust – and exchanged manuscripts before publication, and eventually Wiesenthal too came to meet him here in Heidelberg.

So the star's life had continued on its smooth way. He had published his 'secret' Spandau diaries, which the historian had found so fascinating, another publishing success. And that is how they had ended up here talking about all this and, having reached the end of their conversations, she threw in a strange but shrewd remark: 'I think I know what you knew about the Jews.'

She had chosen her moment well. He was tired after three weeks of explaining his life and work. He liked doing it, it was stimulating, but it had worn him out. She couldn't gainsay that. He was genuinely worn out by this vision of tortured Jews.

He replied that he could sense that there was something terrible going on in relation to the Jews. She believed him. But if he sensed it, he must have known it, yes? In the end, he gave her a letter he had written to a South African Jewish organization which had approached him to help counter claims by a denialist. It was dated the previous year. In it he reaffirmed his guilt as a leader of a criminal enterprise and the truth of the extermination of European Jews, and he added: 'My greatest fault was my tacit acceptance of this extermination.'

She found these words extraordinary. She immediately put them in quotation marks, seeing them as the clearest possible admission that he could have written.

He had known and he had never accepted that he knew. He had known in the autumn of 1943, perhaps even earlier, and he very soon became ill, unconsciously eaten up by the terrible consequences of his collaboration should Germany lose the war, coming close to dying in 1944, and then he began to disobey his Führer while continuing to serve under him, an increasingly dizzying balancing act. True, he didn't choose to disobey because of the Jews but because of his guide's condemnation of Germany. Nevertheless, he felt an unease that the defeat and the Nuremberg trials, with their testimonies and films, had set off: a survival reflex, which was nevertheless sincere. And so he came up with this argument about collective guilt and individual innocence, a way of saving face, whatever the verdict, not only in relation to others but also in relation to himself. He had survived, written books, been scandalously rehabilitated according to some, an injustice or a betrayal depending on how you looked at it, but his balancing act hadn't stopped, far from it, it had become more precarious with each occasion, each publication, each intervention on his part, and these were permanent, since he was now in a loop of perpetual repetition concerning his years with Hitler.

She saw a battle going on between the two sides of his nature, his battle with the truth, or more precisely against it. He had known but he didn't accept it. She was sure he was suffering, perhaps like no one else she had met, but this suffering was recent, and alongside this it was a stronger and more durable facet of his personality that prevailed, which she couldn't really grasp, confronted as she was by its inherent mystery, but which made him a typical member of Hitler's inner circle.

And when she read these closing words in this letter addressed to the South African Jewish organization, where he admitted that his greatest fault was his *tacit* acceptance of the extermination of the Jews, she thought to herself that at Nuremberg that would have been enough to send him to the gallows.

56

London, November 1980

The historian received a strange letter from the star. He was fiercely critical of the form and content of an article she had written two years earlier in the *Sunday Times*. She was confused. He hadn't batted an eyelid at the time, he had even read it before it was published. They had been talking on the phone since those days in Heidelberg, had discussed writing a book together, a series of portraits of Hitler and his inner circle in two parts, as he saw them during the Third Reich, when he was one of them, and as he saw them now.

This retrospective disavowal was not like him at all. He had always been able to control his emotions and communicate them rationally, too rationally, especially his guilt, a significant proof of the double nature she ascribed to him. In this letter, it was the other way round: the personal disappointment, the feeling of injustice and betrayal, the unchecked and violent expression of his feelings overrode his arguments. He justified himself in a way he had never done before. He brought up the Nuremberg trial and his verdict in order to work out a grudge. He had served his time, assumed responsibility and had nothing more to explain about anything, especially to her, the historian. He had known nothing about the exterminations of the Jews of Europe before the trial, he had said it, again and again, and that was that. He accused her of siding with his detractors, not him.

She phoned him and asked him what was going on in his head, and to her great surprise he was in a good mood. She mustn't worry herself about his fit of bad humour, there was a reason for it and it had nothing to do with her, but he couldn't talk about it.

He was being very mysterious and teasing about this reason, and he wasn't at all like the person she had always known. He actually seemed happy.

She stuck to her guns, and now it was her turn to get emotional. She threatened to end their writing collaboration if that was his opinion of her. So he calmed her down again and promised to see her soon to explain everything.

Living with Him

(1981–)

57

Some people stay single and others live as part of a couple, getting up and going to bed with the same person, and though this is an everyday phenomenon, it has an impact on your personality, as such experiences are never neutral.

There are also cases where your job brings you close to someone, a public figure you are obsessed with, and you end up living with them as much as, if not more, than your actual partner.

Of course, your choice of person will dictate the tone of your days, and how optimistic or pessimistic your worldview is.

You study history, you specialize in a given period, you specialize in the Second World War, you do a doctorate, you become a specialist in the Third Reich, you spend so much time with its leaders and victims.

For example, you are a British historian, you have become a specialist in Adolf Hitler, and every day you get up and go to bed with him, for your whole life. And this situation, where you devote your existence to that of Hitler, is as exciting, fascinating and terrifying as its subject.

Living with him, Adolf Hitler, and living with them, the members of his inner circle, and consequently with their subordinates, the sadistic minions who have become famous through novels, movies and documentaries, is not the same thing as living with Louis XIV or Henri III, for example, if your specialism was the Bourbons or the Valois.

This bears no comparison with your studies of the wives of SS members and the female members of the corps of the SS, or learning day after day that some of them wandered round the ghettos where their husbands worked with a bag of sweets in one hand and a revolver in the other and that they offered a sweet to any child that approached them before sticking the barrel in their mouths to blow their heads apart.

You study history, you specialize in the extermination of the Jews of Europe, maybe some members of your own family were deported and never returned, you are a Jew or you are a Gentile and every day you get up and go to bed with them and the atrocious circumstances of their death. You also get up and go to bed with their executioners and you have no choice, someone has to do it to keep the memory alive.

But we need a historian of the historian to assess the consequences of their specialization on their everyday life, what it is like to live day and night not just with millions of dead people, which is a painful celebration of their existence and their memory, but with the constant sadism of their executioners.

The historian had lived her whole life, from morning until night, with executioners and their victims. Her subject matter was the Nazis, adolescent serial killers and sexually abused children, three different worlds, three passions that had informed each other since she came of age in Vienna in March 1938, that intellectual hub and repose of the last Judaeo-Christian splendours of Mitteleuropa. She had internalized so many documents that she could cross-reference them automatically, creating links worthy of cinematic montage, comparisons that novels use to create effects of terror.

You Are the Führer's Unrequited Love

Except that in this case the stories were real, furnished by real life, which gives them a particular meaning, and the sensation of living on the outskirts of Hell.

One day, she wrote about one of the most celebrated scenes of the Second World War, fetishistically reproduced by cinema, which is actually based on some German newsreel footage shot a month earlier during a similar ceremony. This was cinema doing what in literature is known as paraphrase, collage, quotation, intertextuality, when you cut or rewrite extracts from another work into your own. It was the scene from April 1945, just before the end, when Hitler left the bunker to congratulate some boys from the Hitler Youth. He patted their cheeks, shook their hands, smiled and looked at them with eyes made even more exophthalmic by illness.

And in parallel with this, the historian described another scene that had come to light only towards the end of the 1980s, and which most of the world is unaware of even now in the twenty-first century, despite that discovery. It is curious how we remember some things and not others.

The two scenes played out at the same time in separate parts of the Reich. And this is how they went:

At virtually the same moment that Hitler was stroking the cheek of a boy from the Hitler Youth in the Chancellery garden that afternoon, a column of trucks from Neuengamme concentration camp was pulling up in front of the empty school on Bullenhuser Damm, in the north of the city. Twenty-six men, two women and twenty-two children got out of the vehicles.

The children, boys and girls, of various nationalities but all Jewish, aged between four and twelve years, had been guinea pigs for 'medical experiments' at Auschwitz. A few months earlier, when the camp was evacuated, they had been transferred to Neuengamme, which was considered to be a suitable location for the continuation and even completion of these 'experiments'.

Time had run out. The SS knew that they constituted living proof of their terrible crimes. And so, on that April afternoon, they drove them to the large gymnasium of that school, where they had set up nooses at regular intervals of two metres, and they hanged them.

She also described how the SS had hanged the nurses and adult prisoners too.

This symmetry begs every possible moral question, it arouses disgust and horror, but such reactions do not prevent the persistent occurrence of such events throughout history, meaning that here young kids who would doubtless be killed by a bullet or a shell were being congratulated by their Führer, accompanied according to sources by his beloved architect – he talks about it himself in his memoirs – while elsewhere other kids between four and twelve were being hanged, having experienced nothing but cruelty in the medical torture block of Auschwitz.

Some kids returned to combat, others were hanged, the Führer celebrated his birthday and committed suicide ten days later, hours and days turned into legend by historians and film-makers, and the architect continued his journey through the ruins and reconstructed himself.

Some lived well, the others badly; some were favoured by destiny, chance, birth, others were unfortunate for the same reasons; some passed from one pole to the other, some had the strength to get out, others didn't. These are clichés and in the end, confronted by the ignominy of a situation, there doesn't seem to be any other way to describe this simultaneity of the fortunate and unfortunate. Understanding, sociological explanation and even revolt falter before this relativity, this simultaneity, repeated over the course of centuries in every corner of the world and under all regimes, where some suffer and others rejoice. And pessimism becomes the only wisdom.

58

London, August 1981

It was late, the telephone rang, Don picked up and began to smile. He passed the receiver to his wife. The star was unrecognizable. He had always liked drinking a few glasses of wine to unwind, but now he was completely drunk. Not so drunk that he was slurring his words and drooling, but he couldn't contain his joy.

'What I wanted to say is that, in the end, I don't think I did too badly. After all. I WAS Hitler's architect. I WAS his minister of armaments and war production. I spent TWENTY YEARS in Spandau, and when I got out I MADE a good new career for myself! Not bad when all's said and done, eh?'

She was too taken aback to realize that he had just shown her a true version of himself, a self-portrait of how he really saw himself, proud of his role alongside Hitler and proud of his current role as his opponent, brushing aside or at least relativizing the moral morass which, in any case, did not apply to a man of his generation, a man of the twentieth century with his roots in the nineteenth, passionate about Darwinian science, technological progress and unlimited individual success without pointless considerations of good and evil and inspiring new men to make a better world.

★

She asked him who was calling.

That made him laugh, and then he admitted that he was currently having a bit of an *Erlebnis* – an adventure, an experience.

Again, he was unspecific, but promised to put that right soon over a decent bottle of something. And he hung up.

59

The adventure was a woman of British nationality and German origin. She was in her thirties. She had written to the star in late 1979 after reading his *Spandau Diaries*, which had made a huge impression on her. She had always been taught to despise German men of that generation, and thus to despise her father, whom she loved. His book had shown her the true complexity of events, the mechanics of destiny, the moral torment of learning that they had been working for a monster without realizing it. She had really admired the author.

The star had replied as he replied to everyone. During her three-week stay, the historian had seen all sorts of people come asking for an interview, which he granted freely, even to the idly curious, the tourists ticking off historical celebrities in the way some visit museums or the sources of the Rhine. The star saw it as his duty, a part of his mission, not to turn away anyone so that he could repeat over and over again his version of the facts.

Margret was of a different mind. For him it was a pleasure to talk about the Nazi period. It exhausted her and crushed her, but he was incapable of talking about anything else. Life with the star was about repetitive evenings devoted to the same subjects, Hitler, the inner circle, his work as a minister but above all Hitler, Hitler, Hitler, putrid ramblings that left his family dazed, dismayed and now keen to avoid invitations to dinner. In fact, with them he was largely silent, aware that they had nothing to say to each other, and he embraced instead this steady stream of new listeners. He was a star after all, the star survivor of the Third Reich.

The young German woman was married to a young Englishman, they had two children, she had acquired her nationality through her husband and, despite her accent, found it easier to be British than German. Except, nagging away, there was always a mixture of thoughts and feelings made up of nostalgia, mourning, guilt, shame and a profound fatigue from carrying all this inside her head, this postwar German soundtrack composed of guilt, shame and anger.

Reading the star had changed everything. This man had freed her from her suffering at being German in the world after National Socialism. He had cured her from her malaise and at least helped her reconcile with her origins.

She agreed to see him. Love at first sight is inexplicable, but that is what they felt when they saw each other.

It was the first time the star had experienced anything like it. It was physical love, a love born of an immediate sexual attraction. He was seventy-five, and the historian avowed that he was still a handsome man, even for a woman much younger than him, younger even than his own daughters.

Women had always found him seductive, but this time he was seduced himself, attracted like never before.

For Margret this was a humiliation. The star loved his wife, no question of that, but it wasn't the same sort of love as he felt towards this young German-British woman. It never had been. She had always supported him, and now he was inflicting this passion on her. Hilde, his eldest daughter, was consternated.

She had empathy. Putting herself in another's shoes was as natural to her as breathing. She put herself in her mother's shoes and also her father's. She was unhappy for her mother, furious towards her father, but a part of her was also happy for him . . .

This man's luck really perplexed her. His capacity, his desire, almost his art of living his life with no thought to any consequences.

The star now had some very unlikely conversations with the very small number of friends he still saw. These were all recent friends, post-Spandau friends. The old ones had left a long time ago, or he had driven them away himself through his silence. He showed his editor some photos of his new girlfriend, described her physical attributes in some detail. He was like a lovestruck boy, something that had never happened to him.

He was astonished that life had granted him such new happiness. 'I had to wait seventy-five years to feel something like this,' he exclaimed. His joy was immense and he didn't hide it.

He had perhaps felt joy like this only once before, but he never talked about it in these terms.

60

London, 7 August 1981

'It's Albert . . . It seems you aren't at home . . .'

The historian and her husband were back from their weekend and had several messages on their answering machine. The first was from the star. He was in London for a televised interview with the BBC. They could have met up, such a shame. Maybe another time in Germany, and she mustn't forget to bring Don.

The second was from another British TV channel, ITV. They were asking the historian to call back urgently to talk to them about Speer.

The third was from Canadian radio. They too wanted her to call back urgently. They wanted her to talk about Albert Speer, now that he had died.

She thought it must be a mistake. The succession of the messages with only a few hours between the star's jovial voice and the news of his death made the announcement seem unbelievable.

He had suddenly collapsed in his hotel room while with his Anglo-German adventure, his *Erlebnis*. He had recorded his TV interview that morning. On screen, he seemed full of vigour, even rejuvenated, he had never been on such good form, at least not since that famous period he never stopped talking about, the

Third Reich, the war, architecture, Hitler. He had mischievously declined a dinner invitation from his interviewer, the historian Norman Stone, telling him he was 'otherwise engaged with a young lady'. The previous evening, they had dined until two in the morning to prepare for the programme. It was as if he were that night owl again, back in the days of those interminable sessions looking over models or plans at the Chancellery or at Berchtesgaden. Life was sweet, London represented the passion of a woman and the aesthetic passion of memory, the present and the past, the artist and the lover, travel too, the best sort of travel, where a short, intense, beautiful stay was a metaphor for a whole life.

He was taken to hospital in the middle of the afternoon. His adventure, his *Erlebnis*, wept constantly. She had witnessed him suddenly lose consciousness. It was she who informed Margret, which the star's family found unbearable.

At 10 p.m. Berlin time, he was declared dead of a brain haemorrhage.

61

Europe, 1981–2012

'In the past I had belonged among those who were most conspicuously honoured, along with movie stars and singers,' he wrote in his memoirs around 1967–8 about a dispute between him and Hitler in early 1944.

This is how he remembered it, in terms of his own image returned to him by another, and therefore in terms of love and its pangs and its hatreds. And he detailed the terrible feeling he had that his guide was drifting away from him, and the anger that this caused him, and the jealousy he felt towards those who were going to take his place, so he thought.

But he hadn't lost his place, the guide had got him to say that he loved him just as much as ever, and he had survived and even become one of those stars he compared himself to. An ambiguous star, but undeniably a star, an object of love and over-the-top hatred which only very few individuals, no matter whether they are good or bad, are able to incite in the vast majority of people who are themselves incapable of arousing such reactions and can only feel them for these rare chosen few and their images.

After his fortunately sudden death, the ultimate example of his lucky star, and since they couldn't write any of the books they had planned on working on together, the historian decided to write about him one last time, not an article this time, but a whole book.

And so she set off on the adventure, the authentic *Erlebnis*, of writing about this star, who had written so well about himself that all biographies of him read disturbingly like involuntary paraphrases, an unsuccessful struggle to reveal the lies of the source text. It always resulted in defeat, the defeat of biographies in the face of autobiography. And if what he had described of his life with Hitler and what he had heard and chosen to ignore concerning the extermination of the Jews, as in that masterful scene where he described how a gauleiter told him never to visit one of these camps in Poland and he elected not to probe further, if even these kinds of confessions were tainted by omissions, exaggerations, distortions of facts when viewed by the winners of history – in the light of everything that was now known about the Holocaust – and sealed his status as the star of German guilt; well, when you actually read them, these omissions and distortions, these carefully calibrated theatrical effects seemed more plausible than the truth itself, the truth unearthed here and there by specialist investigators.

He adroitly weaponized the moral dilemma of every historian, that is, to avoid as much as possible making a posteriori judgements about the periods they are studying. And public common sense would agree with this. But most in the end fall into the trap, and in the case of the Third Reich they fell even more readily, the star had noticed.

He understood that historical science was an art of war, and the historian the last protagonist in these wars that they constantly studied, not an objective person writing from a peaceful era, but a winner or a loser engaged in a battle of stories, someone who chooses a side, even when they claim not to.

Perhaps that is why he calmly, even haughtily, welcomed all those historians who were arguing with him about his past as a 'good Nazi', an expression coined to discredit his memories, and he awaited them without qualms, watched them arrive like totally naive warriors of memory onto terrain that he knew like the back of his hand, his own terrain, the man of total war and the favourite of Adolf Hitler, whom everyone, except for pathetic denialists and dumb nostalgia merchants, now considered as mass murderer number one, the quintessential image of Evil on Earth. How could these historians take on the favoured son of the greatest exponent of mental manipulation who had ever graced the political stage?

It was no small thing to have been the Devil's unrequited love, he who was so well versed in German romanticism, that's what he had tried to say to the historian when he had made his drunken phone call, when he had said that, after all, HE had been Hitler's architect and armaments minister.

And the historian spent fourteen years writing her book, spending a similar amount of time living with him as he had shared with his Führer. But in fact, no, even dead, Hitler was still a fixture in the mind of his favourite. They were a couple, much more than either of them were with their respective wives.

The historian spoke to all the survivors, the ultimate witnesses of their relationship, those more or less close to Speer. She saw Margret and Hilde again. She met that childhood friend and collaborator, guardian of his architectural projects and steadfast support at the time of his incarceration, whom he had completely betrayed.

She met his personal secretary and became her friend, noting her admiration for the man she had served, and all the pomp of their glory days, such as the private inauguration of the new Reich Chancellery in January 1939, her wonder at the splendour of the building, and her fear in late April 1945, when her beloved minister had informed her that he wanted to see their Führer one last time, and the slap she gave him when he returned from the meeting and asked in a jokey mood, 'So, anything new around here?'

She met dozens of people: the editor of his memoirs, the pastor Georges Casalis, the wife and children of rabbi Raphael Geis, still perturbed by their father's friendship with this Nazi, and also the son of Karl Barth, as well as several former SS members and colleagues from his Berlin Bureau of Construction, like Karl Maria Hettlage, the man who had said to Speer that he was Hitler's unrequited love.

She met them all and made them the joint subject of her book, which is not so much a biography as a work of genius, and for that reason the best thing ever written on Speer.

The other subject, the more crucial one, was her visit to him in 1978 and the relationship she had with him during and after their encounter. That was her stroke of genius: not the umpteenth biographical work but the story of a relationship between a historian and the object of her study who happened to be still alive, the amazing simultaneity of two times that are normally separate: the lived time of the historic characters and the later time of the historians and their accounts. Professional and personal motivations ended up intermingled. Then something else began between them, a novelistic experience. The lucid historian in search of evidence became confused with another figure, a less and less lucid friend, a confidante of the contradictory stories of a person who had been associated with evil, and whose aura, she readily concurred, derived from this association and made him quite magnetic, with his tall, slim figure, his politeness, his erudition, his moral dilemmas. She had read his memoirs and his diaries, and for three weeks she had got him to talk about what he had experienced and what he had written and said about this experience, and now, alone with her own memories of him, she kept coming back to it, memories upon memories upon memories, a dizzying, infinite hall of mirrors.

You Are the Führer's Unrequited Love

And without quite realizing it, as narrator, she became in turn a character in this story, a story that was as truly astounding as it was enigmatic.

She came up with a good title for her book, which was published in 1995: *Albert Speer: His Battle with Truth*. But when you read it, and saw her in it from the start, Speer's battle was reflected in the historian's battle with the stories he was telling her. A battle against and with all his successive avatars, the architect, the minister, the prisoner, then this enigmatic star before her; a battle against his writings and his statements; a battle against his truths and his fictions, at least a certain form of fiction. And to finish, a battle of the historian with herself and her own motivations, wanting to pierce the enigma of this man and empty him of all his fascinating substance but instead reinforcing it, and being sucked into this relationship between him and Hitler, becoming yet another character in the story.

62

2012 and After

Gitta Sereny died on 14 June 2012 in Cambridge. Some tabloids laced their obituaries with venom. Because of her professional interest in Nazism, teenage murderers and sexually abused children, which spilled into her private life and led her to assiduously visit the subjects of her studies such as Mary Bell and Albert Speer, becoming friends with them, she was seen as a troubling, ambiguous woman, fascinated by the Evil she was constantly exploring. She hid her Jewishness, they insisted, by converting to Catholicism. She hid the real reasons for her flight from Austria, when the Nazi students in her drama class kicked her out because she was a Jew. She rehabilitated murderers in her own way. She did not accept that the extermination of the Jews of Europe was utterly distinct from other atrocities of history. These accounts were full of venom, based on lies and simplifications, and the historian was dead, unable to defend herself. She seemed to be on the receiving end of what the star had warned her about previously, namely that 'It's dangerous... to say anything positive about the men of that period. Because it is always taken as admiration or approval.'

And she had been the witness and observer of the events she recounted not as a chronicler, a memorialist or a novelist, but as a historian, implying the moral rigour that the discipline is meant to possess, based on the search for truth.

You Are the Führer's Unrequited Love

She had lived experience of all of this, and from this point of view the 2020s and the 2030s will be crucial decades.

They will see the last of their kind, the victims and executioners, the combatants and civilians, old enough at the time of the events to remember this war unlike any other.

When they are gone, there will only be history and literature.

63

Now, it would be tempting to add the last piece to the chessboard of this story, the one which, more than any other, depends on who is telling it and how it is told.

The missing piece is the novelist himself.

It would be logical for the author to follow in the footsteps of Albert Speer and Gitta Sereny in revealing his stagecraft. That was after all how it all began: the illuminations, the anti-aircraft spotlights shining into the sky of Germany, a dome of light unsettling and enchanting its audience, a mixture of theatrical kitsch and ethereal architecture provoking excitement, disgust, contemplation, trance, imprinted for ever on the collective imagination.

And honesty demands that the real author insert himself here, in the first person singular, just before the end of his own book.

But it is worth restating: this is a true story tinged with falsehood, told by a main character convicted of war crimes and crimes against humanity in Nuremberg, who escaped the death penalty to produce, in *Inside the Third Reich*, yes, his memoirs, but more accurately a compelling fiction about himself.

These days, we would call it autofiction.

*

So, with this understanding of what he did, it would have been tempting to go back to the beginning and imagine a sort of self-portrait with Speer, retracing the path that led me to him.

I read *Inside the Third Reich* around the age of twenty-five. Over the years, I have returned to it many times. This was not by chance. Since I first discovered his story, Speer has struck me as an extraordinary character for a novel. I considered writing something around the relationship between politics and art, the seduction of power and compromises that the artist makes with it.

However, I failed to write that novel. But the more I failed, the more this figure of Speer and his relationship with Hitler obsessed me. Like most Europeans I have complex family links with the Second World War, though in the present context they are irrelevant. When it comes to literature, I have never thought that personal motivations, even the most painful ones, were more important than imagination in the strictest sense or that these gave you more legitimacy to write about yourself than an author without your experience.

And so without realizing it, I entered into Speer's narrative game. After all, it wasn't for nothing that he and Hitler had made up the last of those pairings that are so characteristic of European culture, the artist and the statesman, a reprehensible caricature of Michelangelo and Julius II.

It was only recently, during my umpteenth rereading of his memoirs and the umpteenth rereading of many of the biographies that followed, that I understood why it was impossible to write fiction about Speer.

He had written his own novel, with all the seduction that implied.

What he had created, not only in his own books but also in the evidence he gave at his trial at Nuremberg, was the autofiction I have just mentioned.

Jean-Noël Orengo

Or more precisely, since there are both *positive* and *negative* near-death experiences, *negative* autofiction. The opposite of literary autofiction as we know it. A political autofiction all the more radical as it was about Nazism.

He had first given it aesthetic form in stone, through his architecture and his rallies. Then, even more decisively, he had done it in his writings.

I began to see Speer as representing a wider and very contemporary phenomenon which we experience every day when we open our newspapers or log on to social media. Fake news, conspiracy theories, alternative facts, competing narratives, the normalization of wrongdoing, self-pity, the glamour of anger, the undermining of meaning. Who writes history, and above all, how do they write it? Who has the right to write, who is the most qualified to write? The main protagonist – perpetrator or victim – or a person extraneous to the story – the novelist, the historian?

And which is the most seductive? Truth or fiction?

Speer embodied these questions more than anyone else. He had always lied. He had lied, but he had given the best version of himself, despite or even because of his omissions and his spectacular autobiographical inventions. Historians proved long ago that his memoirs are a skilful tissue of lies. He lied at Nuremberg. He had known about the extermination of the Jews of Europe. He had even participated in it in his capacity as minister of armaments.

Deep down, I told myself, even at his trial everyone knew that he knew about the extermination of the Jews. How could the minister of armaments, who used deportees from the camps in his factories, be unaware of it?

*

You Are the Führer's Unrequited Love

So the main question did not implicate Speer. It implicated his public. It implicated us. How could we have ever imagined that he didn't know? Why had we thought that? Did we prefer his version of the facts to those produced by so many historians over successive generations?

Therein lay the major interest of this story. How had his judges come to believe him, and how, later, despite all the revelations about him, had Simon Wiesenthal and Raphael Geis chosen to believe him too, and even become friends with him?

These questions touched on the powers of fiction, the meaning it assumes in our lives, which only literature could, not elucidate, but attempt to expose in their fulness. Saving your skin through fiction, autofiction, storytelling, whatever, as long as it is *written* or *spoken*.

The Scheherazade syndrome. There is of course the Stockholm syndrome for the victims, the Stendhal syndrome for those struck down by the journey. Fiction deserves its own.

Germany, 1933–1981: being an essential cog in a genocidal regime, then pretending to know nothing about it, saves you from the noose, and then, even better, allows you to climb your way back up in postwar society and become a star of German culpability.

That has been my domain since I don't know when: the Scheherazade syndrome.

A different type of book occurred to me. By considering Albert Speer as the author not merely of falsifying memoirs but of the most radical aesthetic and political autofiction ever written, I found a guiding theme and a dramatic arc: the emergence of an extraordinary lie and a total war between Fiction and Truth.

★

Now, I could list all the objections against my project; they are fascinating, they illustrate this after-time which I spoke about, when there will be no more witnesses to tell of the deportations, the forced labour, the medical experiments, the gassings and cremations.

First, people say they've 'had enough' of all these books about the Nazis. I am perfectly well aware that people have 'had enough', aware of the virulent, mocking, desolate hostility towards this cliché of still writing about the Nazis; aware that people think that they know everything about them; they feel they have been force-fed Nazis through novels, documentaries, essays for so long now and they want to move on to something else; aware that to write about a Nazi is to bring him back to life, while so many Jews will not have their name recorded anywhere, despite efforts to find them again; aware that people are less embarrassed about being fed up with it all and groan at this painful memory; aware that it is a depressing, nauseating, disgusting business to get up every morning to write yet another book about the Nazis; aware that it is no longer fashionable, that the former Soviet Union, for example, has become sexy in literature because of Putin and Ukraine, and what is going on in Russia, or even in China with Taiwan, is like a breath of fresh air compared with the Nazis. Phew! Finally! So long, Hitler! Even though, from Moscow to Kyiv, people are still calling each other Nazis, and on French radio, in the context of the Israel–Palestine conflict, a Jew can see himself accused as a 'Nazi without a foreskin'.

And then there is the famous Godwin point, trotted out any time anyone mentions Hitler and the Nazis. A way of shutting down debate. It could almost be the name of a gambit in chess. A favourite board game of the newspapers or TV or university debates. The rule? Anyone who refers to Nazism in relation to some current problem has lost. *Reductio ad Hitlerum*, the great philosopher Leo Strauss called it. Fallacious reductionism. A vegan and anti-speciesist Hitler – loved his dogs, despised the meat eaters in his entourage. A Hitler woke before his time – loved eating vegetables, burning books, using -isms to describe race, sex and the economy. Hitler, Hitler, Hitler . . .

But I ignored these jaded objections, I signed a publishing contract, I was fortunate enough to do so.

A sort of pact, in fact. A very common one, for sure. So banal it's boring. But don't get all metaphysical about it. Don't compose some textual symphony – a genre much loved by novelists on the Nazis, replete with ostinatos – musical motifs furiously repeated – and draw scabrous, vulgar correspondences between the editor, the dictator, the author, the architect, the artist and his relationship to power, whoever it may be.

Nevertheless, I signed a Faustian mini-pact. Or a mini-Faustian pact. A *faustino*. A *faustinato* with signature and initials at the foot of each page.

And as for the objectors to my book, the Nazi-jaded, in the end I just shrugged my shoulders. As for those who sneered at yet another book on the Nazis and said we must move on, in the end my view was this: it is the Third Reich that reminds us of itself. It is the Third Reich that doesn't forget us.

The Third Reich doesn't forget us, and as long as there are still human beings, it will never forget us. It was designed that way. To make itself unforgettable by the sheer scale of its crimes and the excesses of its monuments. Crimes and monuments.

★

Its aesthetic won the war. It lost the war of arms but won the war of signs. And the conflict continues on the moral and artistic level, a never-ending total war.

Every kid on earth now knows who Adolf Hitler is. They know the Nazi salute and the 'Heil Hitler!' Most people do it at least once in their life, as a game, to be provocative. Some adolescents in their thirties, forties, sixties still do it even now. From Algiers to Tokyo, Damascus, Mexico, Bangkok, Tehran, the Middle East, Africa, Asia, the dark side of the moon, everyone knows the SS uniform, the swastika armband, the leather, the torchlit parades, the Panzers, the Stukas, Hitler and even Göring, Himmler, Goebbels, a quartet from the history books turned into figurines, video game, filmed, graphic or written biopic, alternative histories, S&M gear, Wehrmacht helmet and heels, fishnet stockings, fashion, rock, the quenelle gesture, swastikas, young people revelling in the double S, Wolfsangel style, the Azov regiment, battalion, company, tank columns on the console and on the steppes, Eastern front for ever.

On the other side, unless it's a relative of yours, coming up with the name of a deportee is more complicated. For most of them, it's a very eloquent concert, a long silence, the orchestra pauses, searching, finding at best only the name of a camp – Auschwitz – and first and foremost, *signs*: a yellow, six-pointed star sown onto the chest, numbers tattooed onto the lower arm, striped pyjamas – a binary alternance here too, the flipside of the anti-aircraft searchlights – emaciation, white, bony anatomies, an image floating on the surface of commemorations that become increasingly abstract as the last of the deported pass away, and anonymous, where the human being, the Jew, becomes simply an element of the Nazi décor.

But a proper name?

★

The ancients practised *Damnatio memoriae*, but not the moderns. The ancients practised damnation of tyrants through forgetting, they removed their names from the annals and the monuments, forbade them being uttered out loud, tried to eradicate them completely, but not the moderns. Such is modern humanity that celebrity operates very much beyond good and evil, and the scale of your crimes assures you of an immortality your victims don't enjoy, and when you recognize this, pessimism is the only wisdom.

Pessimism is the only wisdom, and neither fiction nor autofiction can hold out long in the face of Speer. He manipulated truth in the way that writers of the twentieth century manipulated fiction.

Of all the autofictions I have read, *Inside the Third Reich* is the most radical in terms of its content and its consequences. It is a political and aesthetic autofiction, the best ever produced to this day.

It is about a man at the heart of darkness, a major player in this darkness, making himself the subject of his fiction, whose words, and especially his way of saying and writing them, not only convinced the judges to spare him, when they didn't spare some of his collaborators, but also forged history itself in memorable scenes taken at face value by novelists, filmmakers and even historians, notably the famous fall of Nazism, the last days of the Third Reich, which he flew over in his 'Stork', like an angel, an omniscient narrator, visiting each and every one among the shattered and charred eagles and swastikas, creating an ultimate staging for his Führer, no longer in Nuremberg but in Berlin, no longer on a rostrum but in his bunker, a décor of phantoms and ruins, designed by himself, the theoretician of ruins.

★

There are spectacular effects everywhere. When he met with the gauleiter of Lower Silesia against a backdrop of imminent defeat and had the latter warn him never to accept an invitation to visit a camp situated in the region, 'never, under any circumstances', repeating the words to create an effective cadence full of anguish, because what was taking place over there was a sight 'which he was not permitted to describe and moreover could not describe', he cleverly employs a horrific technique along the lines of 'Be careful! Don't go there, the house is haunted, the terrible things that happen there are beyond your wildest dreams.'

And we are now effectively in a hall of mirrors. We know that it is all about the extermination of the Jews, the gas chambers, the crematoria, the selection process on leaving the trains. We know the moral prohibition concerning how the extermination is represented, the impossibility of entering the gas chambers via a camera or keyboard.

Yet here, in an astonishing reversal of roles, is a Nazi who says it. Not a Theodor Adorno or a Claude Lanzmann, but a gauleiter who died in 1945 and who is no longer around to confirm or deny the statements attributed to him by Speer. So we witness a terrible but predictable phenomenon, the aestheticization of the moral prohibition itself. We witness it as it were off-screen, an implacable illumination in which what we can't see, what it would be immoral to see, becomes a scenic component under the pen of the expert scene-creator Albert Speer.

The 1960s and 1970s were a time of literary experimentation in language and the forms of the novel, and it was around that time that autofiction was officially born. Its creator, Serge Doubrovsky, a French writer, a French Jewish writer who had escaped deportation, defined it in the following terms: 'Autobiography?

You Are the Führer's Unrequited Love

No, that's a privilege reserved for the important people of the world, in their twilight years, and written in a fine style. Fiction, of events and facts that are strictly real; or in other words *autofiction*, where the language of an adventure is entrusted to the adventure of language, freely and without the constraints of the novel, whether traditional or new.'

Albert Speer was a powerful figure in the world, in the world at its worst, and yet he did not write an autobiography in his twilight years but, in anticipation, an autofiction on his release from prison. He entrusted the language of his adventure with Hitler to the adventure of a falsely factual language with rhetorical flourishes that render the truth fragile, shifting, tortuous, a grey substance, leaving historians perplexed, infuriated and fascinated, while writers and filmmakers are happy to raid its descriptions and a certain crimson-red light on a made-up face, a neoclassical and 'decadent', as it's popularly called, ambience of black-and-white, an immoral décor, hence more than a décor: a vision of the world.

Pessimism is the only wisdom, and in the case of Speer neither fiction nor autofiction hold out for long, he is upstream of us with his experience and his talent for disguising it.

Journalists conduct counter-investigations, and in the case of Speer, it is necessary to conduct a counter-fiction, a fiction that duplicates the one constructed by a historic person from real facts in which they have played a major role.

Albert Speer, counter-fiction.

A battle of stories, a battle of signs, he is always one step ahead. And it is by taking that on board that it might be possible to escape his trap.

64

One more page, a final variation.

The historian and the star were walking in the woods around his house in Heidelberg. He was telling her about his special relationship with Hitler. He said that it was Karl Maria Hettlage, his SS subordinate at the Berlin Bureau of Construction, who had put his finger on the true nature of their bond when, on the way out of a meeting, he had said: 'Do you know who you are? You are Hitler's unrequited love.'

And he confessed to the historian how happy he felt to hear that.

'I was happy,' he told her. 'Good Lord, I was so happy!'
'Did you feel flattered?'
'Flattered? Flattered? No! Drunk with joy!'